Andriana Ierodiaconou

The Women's Coffee Shop

a novel

Copyright Andriana Ierodiaconou 2012
all rights reserved

Andriana Ierodiaconou asserts the moral right to be identified as the author of this work.

No part of this publication may be reproduced, stored in a retrieval system, or transmitted, in any form or by any means including electronic, mechanical, photocopying, recording or otherwise, without the prior written consent of the author.

This book is a work of fiction. All characters, locations and incidents depicted in it are the products of the author's imagination. Any resemblance to actual persons living or dead, locations or events is purely coincidental.

Chapter One

Everything about Avraam Salih was humble: from his name, which revealed that he was the offspring of a mixed marriage between a Christian and a Moslem and therefore an outsider among Moslems and Christians alike; to the ill-cut suit of a too-bright blue which clothed him; to his condition, which was dead. And not only dead, but unburied - or, to be more exact, unburiable, since a baptismal certificate pertaining to the dead man could not be found, yet neither had he ever been seen at Friday prayers.

Someone, nevertheless, sat in attendance beside him as he lay in lowly state on the narrow iron-frame bed which, together with a plain wooden table, two chairs, and a sombre wardrobe of carved walnut that looked unduly luxurious in its setting, made up the spare furnishings of the room. The woman keeping a vigil over the dead Avraam Salih, her brows knitted, was a striking figure: not tall, but full-bosomed and strongly built about the throat, shoulders and arms which, like her broad, high-cheekboned face, were tanned a brown as deep as that of the walnut wardrobe. Her hair, long, glossy and black, was parted down the centre and tightly braided, the braids in turn wound tightly about her head; brilliant dark eyes, a straight nose, and well-defined, full lips which, had they been parted in a smile, would have revealed a set of strong, regular white teeth, completed a physiognomy that was at once stern and sensuous.

The hands resting on the woman's trouser-clad knees, though well-shaped, were those of a worker, the fingernails short and square-cut, the tanned skin rough. She wore a man's khaki trousers and white shirt, sleeves rolled up and collar open at the throat; her feet, on the large side, were shod in the leather sandals favoured by the farmers and fishermen of the region in the hot months. A cluster of finely-etched lines at the corners of her eyes served as markers of her age, which was thirty-nine.

- "Well, Angelou," she said out loud to herself after an interval of silent gazing at the inert body on the bed, "he's pulled off a fine one this time."

Her voice, deep and mellow, held no rancour. She looked closely at Avraam Salih once again, and sighed; yes, he was dead all right. In life the idea of a practical joke played successfully at her expense would have drawn from Avraam a delighted yelp of laughter; but now he just lay there and lay there, looking, Angelou felt, not peaceful, but simply absent - the human consciousness which had been Avraam Salih disappeared, evanesced, gone, leaving behind a mere agglomeration of tissue which, as far as she was concerned, could have been anything at all. She could no more weep over it than over a stone. Yet something had to be done about it; it couldn't simply be left there, with the flies gathering and the carrion birds not far behind.

With a sudden, decisive movement, Angelou stood up and stepped out of the silent room into the glaring sun of the yard outside. An enormous lizard basking on the stone rim of the well a few feet away darted for cover as she walked by.

It was mid-morning getting on for noon, in August. The heat was already beginning to melt the newly laid ribbon of asphalt which ran past Avraam Salih's door and on through the village of Ayia on its way from the island's capital to the cape. The dead man's house, the very first as one approached the village from the capital's direction, stood in open farmland; Angelou crossed the road to where a carob tree gave thick shade to a battered van of inexpertly retouched sky-blue. Each side of the van bore, in plain black lettering, the twin slogan:

ANGELOU PIERI - PEDLAR - 1001 ITEMS
AVRAAM SALIH - SHADOW THEATRE

Angelou gave the writing a flat look; then, climbing behind the wheel and coaxing the van's reluctant engine into life, she headed for the village centre. At this hour, she knew, the priest could be found at the men's coffee shop which, together with the church of the Archangel Michael and a cooperative general store, formed a rough main square spanning the road. She drove confidently and well, ignoring the overworked van's groans and rumbles, easing it from one gear to another with affectionate expertise, dodging chickens and dogs with hardly a pause.

The village, set on a gentle south-facing slope, was bisected east to west by the main road. The older houses, one-storey rectangles of whitewashed mudbrick with flat rooftops and arcaded covered porches running the length of each building, all overlooked the sea, which lay about half a mile from the foot of the incline. The newer ones, ugly cement boxes representing some local architect's notion of cement boxes somewhere else, typically faced the road, to which they were built as close as possible, in apparent expectation of something grander than a fisherman's or farmer's lot soon to arrive down that narrow, snaking link to the capital inland.

The post-independence housewives lovingly cleaning their front steps along the road's length were the first to discern that something, as they swept and mopped and passed leisurely dusters over mock-marble window-ledges. It came, as expected, from the direction of the capital, and it took the form of buses filled with foreign tourists, whose solemn and strangely incurious faces could be seen speeding by behind inviolable glass, as much of a novelty to the village as the village was to them. At first the buses scarcely slowed down on their way through. More recently, though, they had begun to make occasional stops, the passengers clambering out and filling the men's coffee shop with a din of demands for Nescafé and Coca-Cola. A few might wander into the church, and stand gazing with an air of secret knowledge at the smoky icon of the Archangel Michael, with his severe, beautiful face and peacock wings; and that gave the priest and the sacristan enormous trouble, as they had, each time, to interrupt their siesta or the threshing in order to dash over and ensure that the foreign women didn't enter the sacristy, and that everyone going into the church was reasonably modestly dressed - or, at least, not in bathing suits.

Moreover, for almost a year now word had been going around the village that some of the farmers were selling seaside land - and what land! Totally barren marshland or stony scrub where nothing at all could possibly grow - for unheard-of sums of money: funds already detectable in the process of being translated into yet more cement boxes, destined as dowries for the sellers' daughters.

Angelou, speeding by, curled her lip at the fanciful wrought-iron grillwork on the new doors and perimeter railings, variously depicting grape-laden vines, galleons in full sail, or stags at sunrise, and thought of what Avraam Salih used to say about it all:

- "The bare arse saw its first pair of underpants and shat itself!"

And she sighed again; but the memory of a smile lay in the depths of her eyes.

Within a few minutes she was parking the van outside the coffee shop. In its tree-shaded yard, the village priest sat watching a backgammon game, according to plan. He would be waiting to hear the noon news bulletin before heading for home and whatever poor lunch his notoriously tight-fisted wife had seen fit to prepare for him that day. The old man was something of a saint, which was why Angelou held out no great hopes for a breakthrough on the matter of Avraam Salih's burial. He bore patiently, never raising either his hand or his voice, with a bossy and parsimonious wife whose church attendance record was scandalously thin for her position; he counselled against the land feuds, forced marriages and other common departures from moderation and reason to which the villagers were prone.

But there was even more to him than that. The times were parlous; political ambitions and hatreds were running high. Three years into a fragile independence granted only reluctantly and with great malice by the country's colonial masters, the Christian and Moslem communities were being riven apart; there was blood in the air. The Church in all this stood far from neutral, the bishops in their overwhelming majority being adamantly opposed to any reconciliation with the Moslems. Well aware of the fact that none was more militant than the bishop of his district, the old priest nevertheless remained staunchly impervious to the see's message of division. When, in the coffee shop, one of those febrile political conversations began in which pernicious fact vied with pernicious fiction, when he saw groups of village bloods go into excited huddles at corner tables over the latest talk of accomplished, or proposed, or totally imaginary, killings and counter-killings, he would invariably raise his kindly, bespectacled face from the newspaper he was studying and say:

- "The Moslems do not believe in our God, but they are our neighbours; and Jesus said, 'Love they neighbour as thyself'."

Unfortunately for Angelou, the corollary to this right-thinking streak in the old priest's nature was a rigid adherence to ecclesiastical rules and regulations, the slightest deviation from which was to him quite unthinkable, being a sin. So that, when she stood before him and said, with the eyes of the entire coffee shop upon her:

- "Well, Father - are you going to bury the man, or not?" her question was rhetorical and held no real hope.

Everyone, however, stood hushed for the priest's response. They all knew who "the man" was, and what problems presented themselves in getting him buried. When the inevitable answer came, the air was momentarily filled with a sighing murmur. Assent? Pity? Angelou didn't try to give it a name.

- "You see, my child, without a baptismal certificate - " the priest brushed aside her involuntary gesture of impatience and continued steadily, everyone in the room hanging on his words,

" - without a baptismal certificate, there is no proof that he was ever received as a member of the Church."

Then, in the only sign of how much pain the refusal gave him, the old man got up without waiting for his beloved news bulletin and, crossing the road, walked slowly off home, thin shoulders bent, to the crust of bread and morsel of stale cheese that surely awaited him.

- "Father, the news!" someone cried after him; but he was already out of earshot.

Angelou, too, was in motion, on her way back to the van. The patrons had already returned to their cards and backgammon. Normally, the extraordinary presence of a woman in that male domain would have been enough to sustain their curiosity even after the conclusion of whatever business had brought her there; but Angelou's femininity had been discounted by the village long ago. Only the coffee shop keeper, something of a busybody, cared to call out to her as she once more brought the van coughing back to life:

- "Where are you going now?"

- "To the hodja!" she answered and, shifting into first, sped off into the blazing noonday heat as the coffee shop, its attention gripped anew by her response, exploded into remonstrations behind her.

Angelou, driving hell-for-leather out of the village, was well aware of the risks she was taking. More aware than any of the backgammon politicos shouting in her wake, she thought wryly. For one thing, she had seen the stab wound in Avraam Salih's chest, and they hadn't. For another, she was a pedlar, she travelled the area daily, saw and heard things, put two and two together. Ayia and the Moslem village she was bound for had escaped trouble - so far. The road between them was considered relatively safe; and farmers from each tended their land, often closer to the neighbouring village than to their own, undisturbed. But just two weeks ago, in a place not fifteen miles distant, a Christian bus taking pilgrims to the monastery on the cape had been ambushed by Moslems - in retaliation, it was said, for the killing one week earlier of three Moslem men from a village considered particularly hostile to the Christians, driven out of their homes after midnight by masked gunmen and shot in the fields in cold blood. So rumour had it. Truth? Fiction? Some said, lies - a total fabrication by the Moslems. Others said, no, it had indeed happened that way - but the killers were not Christians but Moslem provocateurs. A third group - the few - dropped their gaze and kept their own counsel when the subject came up.

Angelou counted on familiarity as her shield. It hadn't yet come to neighbour killing neighbour; the two sides still felt the need to shroud their deeds in anonymity - the face hidden by the stocking-mask, the nocturnal foray, the shot fired from a hidden position. They weren't yet able to look their victim in the eye, and carry out the slaughter before an audience, openly. The goings-on, after all, were only "troubles"; that is, not widespread enough quite yet to merit the term "civil war". Before the "troubles" began, the Moslem village next door had been a routine weekly stop for Angelou; she knew the inhabitants and they knew her. She drew comfort from that thought as she willed the van up the incline leading out of Ayia in an eastward direction, to where the land levelled off to form a low plateau, covered with windblown myrtle scrub and a profusion of wild thyme. She was at her destination in less than twenty minutes. Her throat dry, Angelou reduced speed, making for the mosque and the hodja's house which she knew stood next door.

The village was quiet; it was the hour of the midday meal here, too, and most people were indoors, or taking their noon break in the fields, where the reaping was in progress. Suddenly, out of nowhere, Angelou saw a man step out into the middle of the street, directly in front of the van. As she braked sharply to a stop, two more men joined the first, one carrying a hunting-rifle. Angelou, her jaw set, followed their movements with half-closed eyes, and waited at the wheel. After a brief consultation among the group, Hunting-Rifle walked around the car to the driver's window.

- "What do you want here?"

- "The hodja. About Avraam Salih." Angelou, her eyes fully open now, looked her questioner in the face. She knew him; in normal times he drove the village bus.

- "What about him?"

- "Dead. Our priest won't bury him."

The man gave her a keen look; then, turning away abruptly, walked back to his companions. Another discussion followed. To Angelou he had spoken the Greek dialect of the Christians; with his comrades he used the Turkish dialect spoken by the Moslems. She understood enough of it to know that they were debating whether to search the van or not.

They were still arguing, when a delighted voice sang out:

- "Angelou - ou - ou!"

From across the street, a fat middle-aged woman in a red flower-patterned cotton dress and yellow headscarf waved at the pedlar through an open window. A moment later she stepped out through the front door and began waddling over to the van, beaming, exposing a mouthful of gold teeth.

- "Angelou, dear, we haven't seen you in so long!" She seemed completely oblivious to the group of men, on whose faces suspicion mingled with irritation as they watched her approach the van.

- "And I've been needing those coffee-cups again - the ones with the gold rim!" Not even pausing at the sight of the rifle held by the man beside the van, she grabbed Angelou's bare arm through the open window with both hands and squeezed it, out of breath with all she had to say. "Welcome! Welcome! My grandson broke two again just last week - "

Angelou, seizing her moment, climbed out of the van and, imitating the fat woman in behaving as though the men did not exist, walked around to the back and wrested the door open by its rusted handle.

- "For you, Zehra... a special price like always!" she said, rummaging around for the cups, the fat woman shaking with laughter behind her.

- "Oh yes - oh yes - my husband too he says, 'For you Zehra, something special' - ...." Her gold teeth flashed, her belly and bosom shook with laughter at her own drollery.

When, a few minutes later, Angelou turned around triumphantly brandishing a cardboard box full of the desired coffee-cups with saucers to match, she found that the fat woman had been joined by two more housewives. They, too, were smiling - perhaps a little more diffident, a little more uneasy over the presence of the three men, who stood, silent and serious, observing the scene - but still visibly pleased to see the pedlar, extending their hands in a handshake.

- "How are you?"
- "How are you?"

And, in a ritual she could - and sometimes did - perform even dead drunk, Angelou began to display her wares, as more and more women gathered around the van.

- "See these? Finest cotton. And these? Plastic. No rusting, no nothing. Just a quick wash and that's it. Don't set it on the fire, mind - "

When she next had a chance to look, the men were gone.

Half an hour later, she was at the hodja's house. The hodja himself, a small man in his sixties with wire-rimmed glasses and a short greying beard, was sitting in the shade of a large fig tree, lunching on a plateful of its sensuous purple fruit and a loaf of bread. When he saw her he got up nervously, obviously startled by her presence. Two conflicting impulses - to send her, no matter how, on her way as quickly as possible, or to ask her to sit down - joined in a visible struggle on his face. In the end hospitality - combined, Angelou guessed, with a healthy dose of curiosity - won the day, and, mustering a weak smile, the hodja invited her to taste the figs. Angelou murmured a polite refusal, but accepted the empty chair he drew up for her. This would take some time.

They began to chat; the hodja asked after his Ayia acquaintances, not alluding to the reason why he hadn't seen them recently, after which they discussed the harvest, which everywhere was poor after a winter of drought. Her host, whom she knew to be a widower, then insisted on making coffee, and withdrew into his simple mudbrick house, emerging ten minutes later with two small cups full of syrupy, scalding liquid and two glasses of cold water on a tin tray. It wasn't until after he had had his first sip of coffee that he finally enquired, with an exaggeratedly casual air:

- "And what brings you here, if you don't mind my asking?"

Angelou chose her words carefully.

- "You know Avraam Salih."

The hodja nodded imperceptibly.

- "He's dead. There is no baptismal certificate. His father came from your village. Could it..."

He interrupted her.

- "His father was from here, true...though no relatives remain..."

He paused for a moment, and Angelou held her breath. But his next words made her heart sink once again.

- "But Ibrahim Salih was not raised as a Moslem. There was no - ahem, excuse me - circumcision ceremony; he didn't attend our mosque, or observe Ramadan. The people here say he was baptized."

The hodja stopped his recitation, and sat observing the lines of tiredness on Angelou's face, the pallor beneath the sunburn. At length he said evenly, not unsympathetically,

-"It is difficult."

Angelou was not quite sure wherein, to the hodja's way of thinking, the difficulty lay; but she appreciated his tone. He was, after all, risking a visit from the three men who had accosted her earlier in talking to her at all. She stood up, proffered her hand, which he shook gravely. They said goodbye, pronounced the polite formulas of thanks for a visit, of counter-invitation, in a tacit refusal to acknowledge the abnormality of the situation.

She drove back to Ayia without further incident. Once more, she parked the sky-blue van under the carob tree across the road from Avraam Salih's house. As she walked into the room where the dead man lay, a long-legged grey cat with green eyes emerged from under the bed with a raucous meow.

-"I haven't forgotten you, Pulcheria," Angelou said, stooping to pet the animal. Then, a frown on her exhausted face, she sat down once more beside the body.

She had known it would come to this in the end. Going to the priest and the hodja had merely been part of a necessary ritual. The same ritual that had prompted her earlier, as soon as she had determined that Avraam Salih was well and truly dead, to make straight for his grandfather's house. After an eternity of banging at the enormous wooden portal, behind which lay the courtyard and buildings which the old man now occupied alone, he had at last opened up. Grossly fat, completely bald, Hadjimbey in his seventies still preserved a good deal of the presence and malign force which, in his youth, had made everyone fear him - except his daughter, Avraam Salih's mother. But she was dead, and so was Avraam, while the old ogre stood alive before Angelou, cursing through his emphysema, straining to make out the figure at his door with diabetes-dimmed eyes. She had stood her ground, asked her question, but of course it had been no good.

- "If they baptized their bastard, they didn't invite me! Out of here! Out!"

And he swung the huge wooden door closed with a crash. Angelou's efforts had served merely to alert the village to Avraam Salih's death; as she turned away from Hadjimbey's house, she could sense curious eyes spying through neighbouring windows, could already hear the excited murmur of voices.

- "Bah!" Angelou expostulated to herself, shaking her head to dispel the picture of the old man's

meanness and the malicious curiosity of strangers. She tapped her foot, clicked her tongue in exasperation. Yes, she had known it would come to this in the end - that, as Avraam Salih had lived, so he should some day die: a man apart. But at that thought she raised her chin sharply and said impatiently to herself:
- "Enough philosophy!"
Then, rubbing her tired eyes:
- "The thing is, where do I bury him, that's what the thing is."

Shrugging off her weariness, Angelou stood up again. Going back outside, she drove the van into Avraam's yard and proceeded to empty it of its assorted cargo, stacking the boxes, bales of cloth, pots and pans and other paraphernalia of her pedlar's trade next to the well. Indoors once again she walked up to the bed and, with strong, deft movements, wrapped Avraam Salih's body in the thin cotton counterpane on which it lay. Then, spitting into the palms of her hands, she wrested the corpse over her right shoulder. Grunting and heaving, bent almost double, she staggered out to the van, and, in a final effort, half-threw, half-deposited the body on the cargo compartment floor.

The sky-blue van set off once more, this time following the main road in a westward direction out of the village to where, just beyond a small stone bridge, a dirt track branched off southwards in the direction of the sea. After a mile or so, on the border with the sand-dunes which lined the shore, the track petered out among a group of gnarled, windswept olive trees.

Angelou, bringing the vehicle to a groaning, shuddering halt, climbed out and looked about her. This piece of land had come to her from her father, but she had never bothered to tend the trees or harvest their meagre yield of olives. Now she saw that it was destined to serve a grimmer purpose. Extracting a spade from the rear of the van, she began to dig.

The previous few days had seen a series of those violent thunderstorms which, in mid-August, relieve the Mediterranean summer drought; as Angelou plied her spade, the rust-red clods loosened easily, releasing a rich smell reminiscent of freshly-baked bread. She dug in a semi-trance; she couldn't have said how much time had passed as she finally stood, drenched in sweat, by a narrow grave at the bottom of which lay the shrouded body of Avraam Salih. Angelou gazed at it, resting on the handle of the spade. Should she recite something? A prayer? The thought made her frown. After the priest and the hodja had both refused to bury him! No, not a prayer. Suddenly, throwing her head back, Angelou began to sing. Her rich contralto voice filled the space among the olive trees, rising above the monotone layer of sound imposed by the cicadas, floating into the perfect blue of the August sky; her song lamenting, not death, but life. Now, for the first time since she had come upon Avraam Salih early that morning lying covered in his own blood in the dirt, she truly felt his loss; now the knowledge began to burn into her heart that she would never see him again.

As abruptly as she had begun, Angelou cut short her singing and, drawing her shirtsleeve across her nose with a savage movement, began to fill the grave with swift, strong pitches of the spade. When she had finished she drew a pen-knife out of her pocket and, on the trunk of the nearest olive tree, carved: "A.S. 1927 - 1963". She surveyed the initials and date briefly. Her work here was finished. There was nothing else.

Throwing the spade back inside the van, she slammed the rear door shut, jumped into the driver's seat and sped off in a cloud of white dust. Behind her, the olive trees turned to silver in the first breath of the evening breeze from the sea.

Chapter Two

It feels strange to be at the centre of a story. In all my years with the shadow theatre, I never put myself on stage; my presence lay in the philosophical underpinnings, if you'll excuse the pretentiousness of the expression, of each play. Meaning it was hardly registered at all by the majority of the audience, who after all were there for such laughs or thrills as the piece could manage to provide. I like to think there were always a few of those. But they won't be missed - never fear. That little box in the corner of the coffee shop with its seductive aquarium of a picture - soon, that will be in every living room; and who'll so much as remember the shadow theatre then? Not even the older ones, who remained stubbornly faithful all through the cinema years. Oh, yes - in more ways than one, it was high time I died.

No matter. Angelou has buried me well, as I knew she would. Where I lie I can hear the sea, which all my life I loved almost as much as I loved Angelou herself; and the olive trees whose roots search out their subterranean life alongside my heart are wise trees, which know that there is nothing new under the sun. For instance, I am not the only one out here, buried without due ceremony outside the prescribed confines of a cemetery wall. No: less than a mile away, at the base of the sand-dunes where it is easier to dig, lies a village woman's miscarried five-month child, which, like my own self, the good priest refused to bury because it had not been baptized. As for the midwife, she was too squeamish to dispose of it. What else could the poor mother have done than to come out here with her husband in the pre-dawn hours favoured by thieves, and mourn and bury the baby - a son, though that shouldn't make any difference - alone, more alone than any human being should ever be? More alone, even, than the jealous man whose murdered wife lies in an orange grove not much more distant, struck down with one determined blow of the spade. When her anxious family, not having seen her for several days, demanded to know where she was, her killer told them,

- "The whore's run off, like I always said she would. I never want to hear her name again."

And the family, who, because he had agreed to forfeit a dowry, had insisted the girl marry him even though he was older than she by a good twenty years, chose to believe him and asked no more questions, either of him or of themselves.

As for those three men rumoured to have been driven out of their homes after midnight and shot in cold blood - they were not three but two, a father and son, and save that they called themselves Christians who their killers were I can't say, but this much I do know: that the two dead men lie in a last embrace at the bottom of a dry well, in a desolate spot where no farmer or hunter is likely to chance upon them any time soon.

Some will no doubt throw up their hands and say:

- "How can God allow such horrors?"

But God has nothing to do with it. I am reminded here of the story of my birth, which, like my death, was difficult. My mother was in labour for three days, which led the spiteful tongues of the village to hiss,

- "She's being punished for defying her father and marrying a Turk!"

When, after the delivery, word of this malicious talk reached her, my mother retorted scornfully,

- "As though God doesn't have better things to do!"

It would never have occurred to her to deny that God existed. The earth, the sun, the moon, humankind, were there for all to see. Someone had to have created them. Who else but God? By the same token, however, she rejected outright any notion that God might be involved in daily life. The architect of the supreme could not possibly also be the arbiter of the petty. Or, as she used to put it,

- "God isn't a farmer's wife tending a yard full of chickens."

After her elopement with my father, she continued going to church on Sundays and holidays, as she had done all her young life. The only difference was that now she didn't walk in shyly after her father and mother, but came alone, taking good care not to look in the direction of either of her parents for the whole length of the service. No one ventured to censure or snub her - no one but her father and mother, that is. Wasn't she after all, despite everything, still Hadjimbey's daughter? Hadjimbey himself may have disowned her, deprived her of the fat dowry which, as the wealthiest man of the village, he had been bound to give his only female child - his only legitimate child of any sex, come to that - but what of it? Blood is blood, and thicker, as everyone knows, than water.

And if she took me along, first as a babe-in-arms and later as a boy who, like the other boys, became impatient with the long services and escaped to run races around the church - still, the old priest was right: I was never baptized. Was it out of delicacy towards my father that my mother made no effort to have me become a Christian? And he - was he returning the favour, in not demanding that I be raised in the Moslem faith? I often wondered, once I was grown-up enough to wonder about such things, whether my father was a religious man. He never attended the mosque - the hodja, too, had it right. Was that because he was a non-believer, or precisely because he was a believer so profound that he felt marrying, so to speak, outside the faith meant having permanently exiled himself from it?

So to speak - because my parents were never legally married. You recall my grandfather's uncomplimentary "their bastard" to Angelou, when she went looking for help in getting me buried. Though I have a feeling he was using the term metaphorically rather than literally. For my grandfather was good at many things: he played a dexterous game of belote, he managed with the utmost success what, in the context of the district, amounted to a small farming kingdom, he was by no means a poor shot; but what he was best at was bearing a grudge. Oddly enough, the grudge he bore in this instance was not really directed against my mother, though she was the ostensible target of his wrath. No - the person he really resented was my father. My mother's transgression, purely and simply, was to have dared to choose her future husband for herself. But my father -

I should begin at the beginning. Picture my grandfather at forty, at the time of my birth. He had by then already lost most of his hair and was shaving the remaining strands, so that his head, massive, round, bald and always hatless, drew the eye in the midst of any gathering, no matter how large. That head, and a year-round paramilitary costume of khaki trousers and shirt, leather belt, and leather boots to the knee, were his trade-mark. His violent temper and autocratic ways were regarded by the village as natural phenomena of the order of bolts of lightning, or earthquakes; one could not eradicate them, one could only try not to be around when they occurred.

That option was not available to my grandmother Lefki, his wife. A plump, white-skinned woman with anxious, slightly protruding brown eyes, she had been chosen by my grandfather not for her looks but for her dowry: over fifty donums of farmland, and a large house. Her family, normally far too well-off to have given a suitor as humble as Hadjimbey the time of day, had agreed eagerly to the match because she was getting on in age - she was nearly thirty when my grandfather married her - and had still to find a proposed bridegroom to her taste.

As it was, they told her Hadjimbey was her last chance, take it or leave it, and painted such a horrendous picture of life as a spinster that she capitulated without a fight. Within a year she had given birth to my mother, whereupon her marriage was effectively over: not only had she failed to produce a son, but it transpired she could have no more children. My grandfather didn't speak harshly to her, or beat her. The poor woman would have preferred that, infinitely - a good hiding, a period of angry looks and sulking, and then a return to something at least resembling normal life. But no: Hadjimbey simply decided that from then on he would ignore her, condemning her to a wasteland of utter lovelessness, utter loneliness, whose sole other inhabitant was my mother.

It was always held, by the village as well as by my grandmother herself, that for his daughter Constantia her father cared not one iota. That may have been true at the beginning, when Hadjimbey's disappointment over the failure to acquire a son was still keen, and when Constantia was not yet Constantia but an infant, a protoplasmic thing in which only a fond mother's sensibility could as yet detect the person-to-be. Later, though, when the baby became a young child, when it began to talk and assert its consciousness, when, not knowing she was supposed to be in exile along with her mother, Constantia would run to greet her father returning from the fields or the coffee shop, and to ply him with droll talk and adoration - then, Hadjimbey began to pay surreptitious attention to her. He noticed how pretty she was, he noticed her intelligence; and, little by little, scarcely admitting to himself what was happening, he grew to love her. By the time Constantia was seventeen - the age when she eloped with my father - she had become the apple of Hadjimbey's eye.

How lovely she was then! Not tall, but with a well-proportioned figure and her mother's white skin; thick, very curly hair tamed into a single waist-length braid, of the same near-black colour as her odalisque's eyes; a little parrot's beak of a nose; and an upper lip whose slight lift and pout lent an indescribable sweetness to the face. Not really resembling either her father or her mother - a culling, on nature's part, of features from among several generations of ancestors, to compose a unique and irresistible whole.

That my father should have fallen in love with her was inevitable, and it is scarcely to be believed that Hadjimbey did not see this coming. After all, he had personally chosen Mehmet Salih to be his right-hand man, and well knew his favourite's character. That is, Hadjimbey knew that Mehmet Salih was as quick-witted as he was industrious; that he was scrupulously honest; and that the one great failing of this paragon was his weakness for women. If, that is, Hadjimbey regarded an amorous disposition as a failing - which, of course, he didn't. Wasn't Mehmet Salih, in fact, a stand-in for the older man the son he, Hadjimbey, had never had? And wasn't it to be expected that this son should be a chip off the old block where women were concerned? Hadjimbey, who had not been near his wife since the birth of Constantia, when he needed a woman simply took one from among the wives, widows and daughters of his labourers without penalty and without a second thought. Christian of Moslem, it didn't matter; they were all grist to his seigneurial mill. The two rules he lived by were, never sleep more than once with the same woman, and never acknowledge any bastards. Rules which Hadjimbey tried to instil in Mehmet Salih, but which, as it proved, my father was far too soft-hearted to abide by for long.

My paternal grandfather, Ibrahim Salih, worked for Hadjimbey as a shepherd. He could neither read nor write, and had such respect for letters that he chose to deprive himself of the help of his only son Mehmet for a good part of each day in order to send the boy to elementary school. At the end of his six years there, the shepherd's son could read, write and calculate as well as Hadjimbey, who himself had not had much more schooling than that. He came to his master's notice when, aged twelve or so, he began showing up at the big house in Ibrahim Salih's stead, to report on the milk or lamb production, or, God forbid, on some disease which might have cropped up among the flock. Hadjimbey was struck at once by the boy's intelligence and even more so by his lively manner, which was quite unlike the tongue-tied servility displayed by the older hands. Over the next few years the master watched the boy grow into a young man, with a sinewy, strong body and a live-wire face whose easy grin and flashing black eyes made him a budding favourite with all the women.

At that time, Hadjimbey himself was approaching the critical age of forty, and had begun to feel the chill wind of mortality blowing about his ears. More and more, he regretted not having a son; more and more, he felt the need to pass on what he knew, of farming, of making money, of life. This shepherd's son was poor, and of the wrong religion; but he was intelligent, energetic, likeable - above all, just when Hadjimbey needed someone like him, he was there.

No one can say whether Hadjimbey's thoughts and plans ranged further than that - whether he recalled cases of Moslems converting to Christianity; whether he thought that in such a case, perhaps, Constantia and Mehmet...I, Avraam Salih, often wondered and speculated, but I can't prove that it was so. It is a fact, however, that when Mehmet Salih turned eighteen, Hadjimbey, amidst general surprise and not a little envy of the young man, assigned him a broad sweep of duties amounting to the position of confidant and foreman. For the boy's true father, Ibrahim Salih, this meant the loss of valuable help with the flocks; but of course, not for one minute did it occur to Hadjimbey to seek the old shepherd's approval.

In his new, elevated role, Mehmet Salih gained not only prestige in the eyes of the whole village, but also frequent access to the big house in which Constantia was being trained in the wifely arts by her mother. It had not been thought necessary to send the girl to school, where she excelled at both letters and figures, for more than two or three years. After that, her budding woman's figure demanded that, for modesty's sake, she remain at home. What need, anyway, did Hadjimbey's daughter have of learning? Her dowry was magnificent; her future assured. Times were changing, it was true; here and there, a peasant's daughter might emerge from the cocoon of her family to train as a school-teacher or a nurse. But paid work was hardly something to which Constantia need stoop.

She was, anyhow, a good girl, and did what she was told. Under her mother's tutelage she learned to weave, make cheese, embroider, and cook; nowadays, if she ran to greet her father as he stepped inside the enormous wooden portal beyond which the world of men's activities lay, it was only to be reigned in summarily:

- "Constantia! Running, at your age!"

And she would stop in her tracks, biting her lip and blushing. Only a slight frown and toss of her braid betrayed how irksome she found this new restraint. Then she would drag her feet slowly back into the house and vent her energy in snatching up one of the cat's latest litter of kittens, tweaking its ears and petting its fur with rough love until it squirmed and mewed for mercy. And Constantia's mother, taking the girl's obedience for contentment, thanked God that in her daughter at least she had no cause for grief or worry.

Bringing Mehmet Salih into the house was like tossing a lighted match into a bale of hay. With their very first crossing of paths, Constantia and the young man felt the invisible current flow between them which binds people destined to be lovers. She would spend her days day-dreaming of their next exchange of glances, living off the memory of it for days afterwards when it came; he began to be haunted, sleeping or awake, by her lovely face.

The first time he and Constantia found themselves in a room alone, it was an early evening in May. She was sixteen; he not yet twenty. Hadjimbey had invited the young man to the house to discuss the wheat crop, which was showing signs of trouble after a series of unseasonable storms accompanied by hail. He called Constantia in, to order coffee; when, ten minutes later, she returned with the laden tray, her father had gone to the outhouse to relieve himself, and Mehmet Salih sat at the big dining table with its embroidered and tasselled cloth all by himself.

As if in a dream, Constantia crossed from the door to the table; Mehmet Salih had not a word to say. Silently, she deposited a coffee-cup next to his arm, which rested casually on the heavy linen cloth, following it with a glass of water from her tray. As she set the glass down, she found herself looking squarely at Mehmet Salih's hand - a young man's hand, smooth and brown, with well-formed strong fingers, idle at that

moment but with something about it of the contained strength of a sleeping jungle animal, which from a state of perfect immobility can spring and attack the split second it scents the passage of its prey. At the sight of that hand, Constantia felt herself grow breathless and lightheaded; and a hot, sweet wave of desire, akin to the glow from quaffing a cup of good wine, surged through her veins. Mehmet Salih said, looking into her eyes,
 - "Thank you, Constantia."

His voice was warm, slightly husky. The sound of it speaking her name gave Constantia another thrill of pleasure.
 - "You're welcome!" she answered, meeting his gaze and holding it for a few moments, during which they read the truth in each other's eyes. Then, turning tail, she all but ran out of the room. She was full of joy. She spent the rest of the afternoon, until her mother's insistent cries called her to supper, hidden in the store-room among wine jars and sacks of flour, savouring her secret alone.

After that, the affair developed quickly. The window of Constantia's bedroom, as young girls' windows will, gave onto the street outside; it was a simple matter for Mehmet Salih to steal up to her house in the dead of night, tap on the shutter softly, and climb over the sill. First love is never cheap, or hackneyed. The emotions powering that most trammelled of expressions - "I love you" - are so authentic and so strong that the words leap luminously from heart to heart in all their essential, marvellous, meaning, undimmed by either world-weariness or guile. Besides which, Mehmet Salih and Constantia were made to be lovers. Each passionate gesture, each word, issuing from the one, found its perfect complement in the other; their lips, their hands, their bodies, met and matched so adeptly and flawlessly that it was as though, just as the ancient philosophers would have it, two halves of a single creature separated by a freak of nature had reunited to form one whole.

- "I love you, Constantia!" He said her name as often as he could, finding it the most beautiful in the world.

- "I love you, Mehmet Salih!" She always called him by his full name, liking the music of it, judging it symbolic of her devotion to the day-time man and all his concerns, and not just to the nocturnal lover alone.

Mehmet Salih had had his first experience with a woman at the age of fourteen, when Lela, the buxom daughter two years his senior of another of Hadjimbey's shepherds, followed him to the sand-dunes where he had gone looking for snails and there proceeded to spend the afternoon showing him what men and women did together and should never have to do without. From Lela he had graduated to a young village widow, bound to remarry but in the meantime making the most of her time alone; followed, when she eventually became betrothed to number two, by a series of fishermen's wives who, by dint of their husbands' absence on trawler-fishing expeditions for days at a time, had more need of Mehmet Salih's company than most. None of these adventures had ever amounted, on his part at least, to more than a pleasant diversion.

Constantia, however, obsessed him; when, as still happened occasionally in the early stages of their affair, he returned to one of his earlier conquests, he found that making love with another woman was like being served plain water when what one craved was wine. He gave all the others up. From now on only Constantia could quench his desire.

His former loves languished, wondered where he had got to, and contrived to run into him in the street alone. One look at him, however, and they shrugged philosophically and let him go. What could you expect from a mere boy? Sooner or later he was bound to meet a minx, fancy himself in love with her, and start sweating and fretting to make her, supposedly, his own. As to the identity of the said minx - well, that didn't take too long to work out. All those officially sanctioned comings and goings to and from Hadjimbey's house! The unofficial ones were bound to follow. Besides, Constantia went to church every Sunday with her parents, and all who had eyes could see what a peach Hadjimbey had in his household now.

Through all this Hadjimbey himself, incredibly, suspected nothing. There came a time when he noticed Mehmet Salih's troubled air, and the dark circles under his eyes; and he slapped the young man on the back and chuckled,

- "A difficult one, eh?"

but Mehmet Salih's awkward silence passed him completely by.

As for Lefki, who had never been in love and was incapable of entering imaginatively into any state which she had not experienced directly, her daughter's ecstatic face and abstracted moods triggered her mother's sixth sense in no way. Mehmet Salih and Constantia were as free to pursue their love as if surrounded by the deaf and the blind.

Of course, things couldn't go on in that way forever. Constantia was content enough; she kept her feelings to herself by nature, and the need for secrecy did not prevent her from being happier than ever before in her young life. But Mehmet Salih's open personality made him ashamed of the deceit towards Hadjimbey, nagged him with increasing insistence to bring the relationship with Constantia into the light. So one fine day he told the older man, brutally almost, straight out:

- "I've something to say to you. I love your daughter!"

They were in the courtyard of the house at the time. Lefki and the live-in maid-servant heard Hadjimbey's roar, thought the building was on fire, and came running.

- "You dog! Bastard's bastard! Son of a whore! Get out! Get out!"

Hadjimbey was brandishing a horse whip which he had immediately grabbed from the stables; he was livid with rage. Mehmet Salih, characteristically, was more concerned about the older man's well-being than his own. Fearing that Hadjimbey, quite corpulent by then and even under normal circumstances explosively florid, might work himself into an apoplectic fit, he was trying to calm him, not with words, but as one tries to calm an animal, with soothing noises from deep within the throat. As he did this he ducked and dodged the horse whip, which Hadjimbey cracked this way and that, trying to strike his erstwhile favourite down. The two women, now joined by a silent, wide-eyed Constantia, stood on the side-lines, wringing their hands, calling on God and the Virgin to make Mehmet Salih obey Hadjimbey and get out. But the younger man, continuing his crazy dance around the horse whip, had clearly decided to stand his ground.

God and the Virgin then did intervene, in their way. Hadjimbey, in running into the stable to get the whip, had been in such an unthinking rage that he had forgotten to pull the door shut behind him as he came back out. Now his chestnut mare, terrified by the noise and shouting outside, suddenly stampeded into the courtyard, rearing up on her hind legs and neighing, threatening to trample contestants and spectators alike. Before the superior necessity of containing the animal, Hadjimbey was obliged to divert the horse whip elsewhere, and institute a pause in his anger. In the midst of the fray Constantia, who had not taken her eyes off Mehmet Salih for a second, found the opportunity to open the large wooden portal leading to the street, and push her protesting lover out.

- "Come with me!" he begged breathlessly.

But she shook her head, kissed the palm of his hand, and slipped back inside. She knew what was coming, and wanted to be there to defend her mother.

As it was, Hadjimbey gave Lefki such a beating for her supposed negligence that the poor woman was obliged to take to her bed for three days; but for Constantia, who tugged frenziedly at his clothes, appealing for mercy, careless of drawing her father's wrath down on her own head, he might well have killed her. On Constantia herself, amazingly, Hadjimbey laid not a finger. She waited a few days, until she was sure that her mother was fully recovered; then, deterred neither by locked doors and windows nor by the maidservant who had been posted to sleep in the same room as a sort of unofficial sentry, she fled her home by night. She was never to set foot there again.

Free, Constantia walked the ten miles to the neighbouring village, and Mehmet Salih's family home. It was almost dawn when Mehmet, who had been undergoing the torments of the damned since his forced departure without Constantia from Hadjimbey's house, heard the timid knock on the door which he had hoped and prayed for since they had last seen each other. Flinging open the door he embraced his love, kissed her lips, her throat, her eyes; she rubbed herself against him like a cat, gazed on him avidly. A shuffling of feet made them draw apart. The old shepherd and his wife had awakened, and stood in the doorway staring. Only then, before their frightened and shocked faces - their son, with Hadjimbey's daughter! What catastrophe lay in wait? - did Constantia finally break down under the strain of it all and, rubbing her knuckles into her eyes like a child, began suddenly to cry.

As it was, this artless display of grief turned the kindly Ibrahim Salih's mood completely around. He began to bustle about, making comforting noises, lighting a fire against the pre-dawn November chill, offering Constantia a bowl of warm sheep's milk, and bread heaped with comb honey; his wife Zeynep, more stiff and formal than her husband before this rich young lady who had stolen her son's heart, went along nevertheless, at bottom proud of what she regarded as Mehmet's conquest. Then Constantia, her face lovelier than ever in the reflected flames, checked her sobs and rested her head on Mehmet Salih's shoulder, once more happy to be alive. She was a child, after all. The complications, the possible suffering which might lie ahead, preoccupied her not at all. Her sole, ecstatic, thought was: "I'll see him again tomorrow, and the day after that, and the day after that. We're never going to be apart, ever again."

The lovers spent the next two weeks in hiding, as the etiquette of elopement required. My mother would always blush whenever, as a boy, I questioned her about that fortnight. To be sure, what I found fascinating was the idea of a grown-up hide-and-seek, and my curiosity was exclusively centred on my father and mother's hiding place - not, as she thought, on their activities there, regarding which subject anyway I arrogantly regarded myself as a jaded expert. Where had it been? I burned to know. Maybe I would have adventures and hide out there myself one day. But she never told me. As time went on, I decided there was only one place it could have been: the caves situated a mile or two outside the village, where an unofficial shrine still exists before which barren women lay down offerings of cloth, wax and clay. There is an underground spring there, and, barely discernible in the grass, the foundations of a chapel; and on the cave walls one can make out the signs of the fish and the cross, clumsily etched by the early Christians who sought shelter there centuries earlier from the Romans' rage.

In any event, for a full fifteen days Constantia and Mehmet Salih were nowhere to be found. The reasoning behind this staged disappearance, central to all elopements, was that at the end of such a period there could no longer be any doubt, either as to the couple's commitment to their union, or as to that union's consummation on the carnal level. In most instances this device then allowed the two families concerned to give in gracefully to a marriage which they had hitherto regarded as anathema, without losing face. No one else would have the girl, now; might as well do the right thing by her, marry the dolts off, and eat, drink and be merry.

In the case of Constantia and Mehmet, however, such a happy ending was clearly out of the question. Everything precluded it, not least the social and religious differences between the aspiring bride and groom. Even if Mehmet Salih had been a Christian, it would have been no easy thing. But a Moslem, the son of a menial shepherd employed by his prospective wife's wealthy Christian father! It was unheard of. Add to that Hadjimbey's notoriously vengeful nature, and the fate of the lovers was sealed.

Knowing this, they didn't even try to petition Constantia's father. At the end of their illicit fortnight they simply returned quietly to her village, and moved into a small house - a hovel, really, just one main room with a tiny pantry-cum-kitchen giving off it - on the outskirts, which some charitable soul who disliked wealthy landowners in general and Hadjimbey in particular had agreed to rent to them for what it was actually worth, which was close to nothing. I was born there, a little more than a year later, one rainy February day. My parents followed the custom, which gave precedence to the paternal grandfather, and named me Ibrahim. They could hardly, in any case, have given me Hadjimbey's name - which, in addition, few knew and no one ever spoke. (It was, incongruously for one so deficient in the Stoic virtues, Zenon).

When my birth was duly registered, the bureaucratic powers-that-be decided that, as Mehmet Salih admitted paternity, my surname should indeed be Salih; but that, as my mother was a Christian and not married to my father, my first name should be recorded in its Christian version.

My mother, seeing "Avraam Salih" written on the birth certificate, was silent for a few moments. Then she said,

- "'A' is the first letter of the alphabet. It's lucky for a baby to have three 'a's in its name."

So I became Avraam, and Avraam Salih is what they called me to my dying day.

Chapter Three

The morning after Avraam Salih's unconventional burial dawned windless and clear. It was almost ten o'clock when, through an open window, a brilliant shaft of sunlight suddenly illuminated Angelou's sleeping face. She stirred; from her parched throat came a groan. She knew she was unhappy a split second before she remembered why. As the memory of the previous day flooded her consciousness in all its bizarre detail, she groaned again. A clumsy movement of her hand sent an empty brandy bottle crashing down from the rickety wooden table at which she sat to its demise on the floor below. From the shadows came a brief, complaining meow; Pulcheria the cat, rescued from her dead master's house, sat in a forlorn half-crouch under a far table, the picture of feline desolation. On the floor next to her a dish of tinned sardines lay uneaten. A glass containing dregs of brandy overturned with another crash on the table-top as Angelou raised the palms of her hands to her face.

- "Aiiiee!" was all she could say. Her throat felt rough and dry, her head swollen to twice its normal size. Red-hot nails were throbbing in her temples.

Gingerly, she pushed back her chair and stood up. The exertion made her groan again but she persisted, directing slow, painful steps towards a gas cooking stove and sink which stood in one corner. With infinite care she took down a small copper pot hanging by its long handle on a nail driven into the wall above the stove, filled it with water, and lit a flame under it with matches retrieved fumblingly from her shirt pocket. From a glass-fronted dresser next to the stove she took a china cup minus its handle; one of the dresser drawers yielded a spoon; a shelf next to the nail reserved for the copper pot, a tin of sugar and one of coffee. With deliberate movements she spooned the dark, bitter-smelling powder and the sugar into the pot, stirred the coffee mixture once or twice, and took it off the flame as it frothed to a boil. Then, armed with the steaming cup, she creaked her way back to her original seat. The whole process, ordinarily a five-minute job, had taken her three times as long.

Angelou took her first, grateful swallow of coffee and sighed deeply; for the first time since she had opened her eyes, she looked about her. She had known this room, with its high ceiling, its blackened beams, its flagstone floor, all her life. She had, in fact, been born in the four-poster bed which still stood against one wall; and it was in that same bed, when Angelou was about five, that her mother had died. She dimly remembered the scene: female relatives moving about, talking in low, sombre tones, and her father sitting by the sickbed, head bowed. She had no recollection of the funeral; perhaps her father had insisted that she be kept at home.

Over the next few years Angelou lived with a succession of maternal or paternal aunts. Some were genuinely kind women, who took her in out of the goodness of their hearts and treated her like a child of their own; others were motivated exclusively by an arid sense of duty, and in their homes she was more of an unpaid servant than a foster-child. Throughout, however, she was able to keep up a regular attendance at school.

When Angelou had completed the six elementary grades, she moved back in with her father. She was twelve. Her schooling deemed finished, she assumed all her mother's former responsibilities: cleaning, cooking, washing clothes. In addition she helped her father, a small-scale farmer, in the fields. The two of them lived together, he growing more and more harsh and taciturn, Angelou more and more eager for a different life, for the next ten years. Deliverance finally came when her father died. She surveyed her situation, and made up her mind swiftly. She sold off what land she had inherited, keeping only a small plot or two near the shore for the sake of a functioning well and a few ancient olive-trees that she was loath to let go; with the proceeds she bought the stock of a small grocery shop in the nearest town, the owner of which had decided to sell up and emigrate. After that, she turned her attention to the house. It consisted of the large room in which she now sat, a store-room giving directly off it, and a yard in which stood a mudbrick bread-oven and an outhouse. Little was needed to convert the main room to the purpose which Angelou had in mind: half-a-dozen wooden tables, a job-lot of plain chairs, and, against one wall, a set of wooden shelves on which items from the defunct grocery - tins of margarine, bags of sugar and flour, spools of thread, Marseilles soap, boxes of matches - jostled for space, and it was done. Outside, above the main door which gave onto a narrow unpaved street, she hung a hand-painted wooden sign which read: "Women's Coffee Shop". Then she waited.

It didn't take long for the first customer to arrive: to be exact, half an hour after she had put up her sign. One of the neighbours, an amiable woman named Katerina with an equally amiable but drunken husband who played the violin at weddings, peered through the door and stepped timidly inside. The two youngest of her large brood of children clung to her apron. Angelou smiled a welcome.

- "Good morning, neighbour."
- "Good morning."   Hesitantly, Katerina sat down. The children looked around, thumbs in their mouths, with big eyes.
- "Coffee?"
- "I don't want to trouble you!"
- "It's a coffee shop, isn't it?   No trouble. Coffee?"
- "If you like!"

Angelou busied herself, deposited a cup of coffee and a glass of water on a table where Katerina sat keeping to the edge of her chair, as if unsure she should be there.

- "And what can I offer you, caca-bottoms?"

The children's eyes grew even bigger; one ventured a smile. Ignoring the please-don't-bother noises being made by their mother, Angelou stepped over to the shelves, opened a tin box, and took out two boiled sweets wrapped in noisy paper, one a vivid green, the other orange. The children began to suck on them avidly, stock-still, as though afraid that moving around would make the sweets melt away faster.

The two women talked of this and that. When Katerina got up to go, she said shyly:

- "How much? If you could charge it till the harvest..."
- "There's nothing to charge. It's free."
- "But you said a coffee shop!"
- "A women's coffee shop. Do women, to your knowledge, have money?"
- "No, but..."
- "But nothing. I said it's free."

Katerina, nonplussed, looked about her, as though for help. Her eyes lit on the shelves; she turned eagerly to Angelou.

- "Do you sell matches?"
- "Yes. One box?"
- "A dozen...if you could charge it..."
- "Till the harvest. I know."

She took a child's exercise-book and a pencil off a shelf, made a mark.

- "There you are. Katerina: one dozen, matches."

Over the next few days, news of the women's coffee shop spread around the village; by the end of a week, only those women who had just given birth or were otherwise bedridden had failed to pay Angelou a visit. Back home, all her customers told the same story: drinks were free; if you needed household staples, Angelou had everything at good prices, and was willing to charge the bill. Their husbands frowned suspiciously, made to object, then realized they had no grounds for it. The women got together to gossip anyway, and the kind of goods Angelou sold were daily necessities. Talking or shopping here instead of there, what could it possibly matter? As long as it didn't mean extra expense! So, but for an initial spate of lewd jokes, the women's coffee shop proceeded to operate without hindrance. In a matter of weeks, it had become the focal point of the village women's social life.

Angelou's motives for starting a coffee shop were mixed: some obvious, others more obscure. Certainly it made excellent business sense, providing her with a ready-made clientele for her improvised grocery business. At the end of each month she was well in the black; the overhead in free drinks - mostly coffee and tea anyhow since, unlike Angelou herself, her patrons were on the whole not hard drinkers - represented just a small fraction of her profits on sales.

But the coffee shop's value to her extended well beyond money. More than anything or anyone else in Angelou's life, the daily gathering of women to drink, exchange news, or quarrel, stood for the family warmth she had lacked since the death of her mother. Marriage, children, represented an avenue which she intuitively felt to be closed to her for life; but sitting in her coffee shop, a little off to one side, over a companionable coffee or glass of brandy, listening peaceably to the rise and fall of conversation, Angelou felt truly at home. Neither her years as a foster child nor the dark period with her father had ever given her this intimate, comforting sense of human contact. If her mother had lived, home would have been much like this - women friends or relations dropping in to sit and talk, argue, tell ribald jokes. Money wouldn't have entered into it - so she could not, would not, charge her coffee shop customers money. Most people of course saw her as just a shrewd businesswoman, said the free drinks were a clever draw for selling soap or flour; and so they were, but not merely. Angelou's entrepreneur's heart was also still the heart of an orphaned child of five; and the coffee shop's offerings were, above all, a bid to recover the love that had disappeared from her life with the death of her mother.

That death destroyed Angelou's faith in a just and ordered world for ever. For longer than anyone knew or cared to suppose, the little girl tried to deny the loss of her mother, making believe that the very next day she would somehow see her again; seizing on a woman's silhouette seen from far away, or on the suggestive shape of a tree, or a cloud, to say to herself:

- "That's my mother!"

Deep down, however, Angelou knew her mother was no longer there. At night, she would lie in the dark hugging herself, her skin aching for a caress, a kiss, offered for nothing, as mothers will offer it, just for love, almost on the sly - almost wanting to hide from the world how much they adore their child. Angelou was physically strong, she grew, thrived even, in the homes of her aunts, and later on back with her father. But her child self lived on inside. Sometimes she felt as though she were two people: one, the outer Angelou, who was grown now, with generous breasts and strong arms and ran a business; and the other, the inner Angelou, small, alone, curled up in the dark, hugging herself and wishing that tomorrow, the day after, her mother would come back and tell her it had all been a mistake, that she hadn't died, just gone away for a while. For a time both selves hoped that there really were ghosts; the presence of the beloved dead woman, even as a wraith, would have been better than nothing.

Angelou's mother, however, was truly gone, and never came back, either as a living woman or as a spirit. The outward Angelou grew used to her absence, would almost have said that she had forgotten it. The inward Angelou still grieved, missing her mother, but she no longer said much, scarcely made her presence known; and this Angelou grew even more quiescent with the opening of the women's coffee shop, appeased by the daily, massed female presence in the house.

The coffee shop keeper was interrupted in her reverie by the sound of the street door latch being raised. A grey shadow streaked across the floor and disappeared into the store-room, as Pulcheria the cat took alarm at the approach of a stranger. Through the throbbing haze of her hangover, Angelou recognized the silhouette framed in the doorway: it was Katerina, her first customer of almost twenty years ago. The jolly young mother of those early days was now a jolly grandmother in her early fifties, grown stout and florid-complexioned. Her eyes, once a clear, sweet brown, were shot through with red veins, and loomed huge behind a pair of ugly glasses with bottle-thick lenses; the beautifully rounded breasts of her youth now hung like sacks of potatoes inside her loose dress of cheap cotton. Age had its compensations, however. Her feckless, violin-playing husband had caroused himself into an early grave, and the bevy of children seemingly permanently attached to her apron- strings were all grown, with small children of their own. Meanwhile, the rise in prosperity since independence had, in Katerina's home, assumed the form of a cheap Italian gas cooker and refrigerator. As she often said:

- "Praise the Lord for everything; but he'd have invented all these machines a lot sooner if he'd had ten children!"

Fond as she was of Katerina, Angelou suppressed a sigh. She knew that her friend was only the first of a crowd of women which was bound to fill the coffee shop before long, hoping for more information on Avraam Salih's death and burial. Indeed, Katerina had hardly deposited her heavy body, with a murmured

"Condolences!", on a chair, when the latch lifted again to admit two more women, their appearance a study in contrasts.

The first, Liza, was a small, plump person in her early thirties, with lively black eyes and dimpled hands and cheeks; the second, Ermioni, was tall and rangy, with enormous, rather other-wordly greenish-blue eyes, a determined line to her jaw, and large raw-skinned bony hands which she held awkwardly, like tools that she had finished using but did not know where to set down. She shared with Angelou the status of spinster, though unlike the coffee shop keeper Ermioni loved men well enough when she chose; she had remained unmarried for the simple reason that, as the fourth daughter of poor parents, she could command no dowry. As, by the standards of the village, she was no beauty, there was little chance of anyone falling in love with her and disregarding that handicap. The option of marrying a widower twice her age with half-a-dozen children she rejected violently, saying:

- "If it's a matter of a crust of bread to eat, I can earn that myself, thank you!"

She then proved as good as her word, persuading the government doctor who held a surgery in the village twice a month to teach her to administer the injections he prescribed. For this service she charged a modest fee; she also supplemented this income by taking care of the dying and the bedridden.

- "Condolences!" Liza and Ermioni murmured in unison, while Angelou waved a hand in a vague gesture of acknowledgement. Katerina sat nodding solemnly, as though in approval of the greeting. Liza, whose husband skippered the trawler operated cooperatively by the fishermen of the village, proffered a covered dish wrapped in a chequered cotton napkin.

- "The captain sends you these - "

She unwrapped the dish, lifted the cover to reveal a generous portion of red mullet that still carried the salt tang of the sea.

- "Thanks, Liza - thanks."

Angelou's voice was hoarse, and she couldn't move from her chair, but her head was beginning to clear as the strong coffee did its work.

- "Sit down, won't you - what will you have? Katerina, Liza – a drink?"

- "Stay there - stay there - I'll do it!"

Katerina got up and began to bustle about, searching out cups and spoons, stirring the coffee as it brewed slowly over the gas flame. Little by little, with Angelou cast in the role of the grieving next of kin relieved of the duties of hospitality for the occasion by thoughtful friends, a kind of wake for Avraam Salih began to take shape. The funeral, such as it was, was over; indeed, those attending weren't quite sure there had actually been a death, having only Angelou's word for it. Nevertheless, the women who continued to trickle into the coffee shop took it on trust that Avraam Salih was no longer with the living. A man, however vagabond his status, not being a dog, some sort of mourning ceremony was required; and they were seeing to it. With each new arrival, there were fresh exclamations of:

- "And such a young man! Who would have thought!"

Then would follow a subdued murmur as the woman was filled in on the official version of the story by those who had preceded her. Angelou, having decided to stick as close to the truth as possible, had disclosed that Avraam Salih's death was sudden, that she had found him stricken down — she did not say by what - in the yard of his home early the previous morning, and that, both the priest and the hodja having proved unhelpful, she had buried him herself on unconsecrated ground. At this last piece of information most of the women crossed themselves with a shudder, whereupon someone would add solemnly:

- "It's true what they say - it's all in a person's fate!"

Only Ermioni, who saw her own life as an educational case of free will trumping God-given destiny, remained aloof from the nods and murmurs of general assent, a faintly contemptuous expression in her turquoise eyes.

The gathering had been in full swing for about an hour when a loud knock at the door made all the women jump. Everyone turned around to see who had deemed such a formality necessary; since the arrival of the first few visitors, the door had been left open, both as a relief from the heat and to allow free access to all comers.

Two men stood in the doorway. Angelou immediately knew the first, who was short and tubby with a small sandy moustache and slightly shuffling gait, to be Mr. Leonidas, the village mayor. It was not until he stepped forward into the light, revealing his uniform, that she recognized the second as the sergeant from the nearest police station, two villages away.

Although evidently bound by a common mission, the two officials made an unhappy team. The mayor was a Communist; that is to say, he believed that all men, irrespective of ethnicity or religion, were equal, and shared a common enemy in capitalist imperialism. He therefore did not hate his Moslem countrymen nearly enough for the taste of the sergeant, who was a Nationalist of the grenades-hidden-in-the-vegetable-basket school, and whose stripes represented a post-independence reward for his role as a guerrilla during the struggle for the overthrow of the country's colonial masters. The setting up of a proletarian state not being one of the liberation movement's stated goals - indeed, the struggle was waged under the triple banner of Religion, Family and Private Property - the Communists felt bound to give it only lukewarm support. That, in Nationalist eyes, made them no better than the Moslems, who opposed the liberation struggle outright, as one that would render them a downtrodden minority in a state run by the Christians. To the sergeant and his fellow-fighters, therefore, liberation was still incomplete: it remained to get rid of the Communists and the Moslems.

The two men who now stood on the threshold of the women's coffee shop represented, as it were, the flotsam and jetsam floating upon the ocean of this complex and unhappy political history. The mayor, stooping a little and not meeting anyone's gaze, looked as though he feared imminent arrest by the sergeant; the sergeant, a tall, not unhandsome man with broad shoulders and a black handlebar moustache of which he was justly proud, glowered from beneath fierce brows, furious that duty had thrown him together with a man he regarded as a traitor. The crowd of women, suddenly quiet, watched and waited in wide-eyed fascination. Finally, the mayor cleared his throat. Expecting an oration, the women leaned forward. When he spoke, however, it was merely to ask, in an uncertain voice:

- "Is there a deceased here?"

Some of the women laughed; others, hearing the word "deceased", automatically crossed themselves. Ermioni cast a questioning look at Angelou, then said curtly:

- "Don't be an idiot, mayor. Do we look dead to you?"

The laughter grew louder; the sergeant frowned even harder. Pushing the mayor unceremoniously aside, he stepped into the middle of the room and called out theatrically:

- "Angelou Pieri?"
- "Here."

Angelou's face was stern.

- "We have information that you have unlawfully buried a citizen without notifying the authorities."
- "Do you?"

Angelou remained impassive. The sergeant glowered. Casting a frightened look at his face, the mayor attempted to soften the sergeant's pronouncement.

- "You see - nobody's saying - but after you came to the men's coffee shop - ..."

Angelou interrupted him, almost kindly.

- "It's all right, Mr. Leonidas. I know what happened, and what the sergeant's getting at."

She turned to the policeman.

- "Look, sergeant, let's get this over with. Somebody came along and told you a tale about Avraam Salih. Well, it's true. He died, and I buried him. No one else would. If there was paper-work that should have been done - fine, I didn't do it. But the fact is, no one gave a damn. If a donkey had died, they would have cared more. So don't tell me I didn't register with this one or get a certificate from that one."

The longer Angelou spoke, the angrier she got; by the end of it she was standing up and shouting. A general cry of approbation rose up among the women.

- "That's right! What should she have done? Thrown him to the vultures?"
- "Women don't know letters! We can't read your certificates!"
- "Why don't you catch some thieves instead of coming here bothering people?"

- "Someone had to bury him!"

The sergeant stood his ground. Still glaring fiercely, he said, in the formal language of police reports:

- "I hereby inform you that an exhumation will be required, followed by a post-mortem to determine the cause of death."

He was in full swing now; the audible gasp that went around the room only made his voice more stentorian.

- "According to the law no person may be buried without a death certificate signed by a physician."

- "So you want me to tell you where I buried him."

- "Exactly."

- "And if I don't?"

- "Then I shall be obliged to charge you with his murder. By your own admission, you were the last to see the deceased alive."

Now there was pandemonium in the room. Angelou attempted to quiet the women by raising her arms, with only partial success.

- "You seem to know all about it, don't you, sergeant? But you can't charge me without a body - what if he's gone to Australia, or England?"

The women, exhilarated by Angelou's defiance, laughed wildly. The sergeant was by now well and truly furious.

- "We'll find the body - never fear!"

- "You lot seem better at making them disappear than at finding them these days!"

The sergeant's face grew suddenly rigid. The mayor turned to Angelou, fearfully.

- "Now, Miss Angelou – please leave politics out of this - "

The room had gone dead quiet. Even Angelou herself looked a little awed, like a child that has involuntarily gone too far and knows that retribution is now inevitable. Forcing herself to speak, she said with a stiff tongue:

- "Just making a joke. All right. I'll show you the grave. The man's dead, one way or another."

Through clenched teeth, the sergeant said:
- "You're lucky I'm not hauling you in for - "

Without completing the threat, he turned around sharply and marched back outside. Angelou, sighing, patted the distraught mayor on the back. Together, they followed the sergeant to the street. Over her shoulder, the coffee shop keeper called:

- "Last one to leave close up!"

The sergeant, looking straight ahead, sat waiting in a police jeep, a constable at the wheel. Angelou and the mayor climbed into the back. Ermioni, peering through the window, saw her friend lean forward to give the driver directions; then the dark blue jeep sped off in a cloud of dust. One by one, the women began to drift off home. Katerina, left alone at the last, debated with herself whether to wait until Angelou came back and offer to cook some lunch; then, thinking better of it, she carefully re-wrapped the plate of fish, placed it neatly in the middle of the table nearest the gas cooker, and left. As she closed the door behind her, Pulcheria crept out of the back room, sniffed the air investigatively, and, finding someone had cleared away the scorned sardines, took up a strategic position under the red mullet. She was not a thieving cat; Avraam Salih had taught her that there were times when the best thing to do was wait.

Angelou sensed there was something wrong the second the police jeep had rattled to a halt in the silent olive grove. Stretching out from the meagre pool of shade under the tree bearing the dead man's initials, the deserted landscape shimmered in the midday heat like a mirage. That was it - the place was deserted; there was no one there, dead or alive. As the constable took out a spade from the car and began to dig the still-fresh rectangle of soil, Angelou shook her head. Forty-five minutes later the sergeant and the mayor, provisionally united in bafflement, stood peering down into an empty grave.

Chapter Four

Introducing Zenon Hadjimbey - that was always rewarding. All I had to do was trot out a fat, bald figurine wearing boots, and the audience would instantly erupt into boos, jeers and whistles. He was the easiest character to perform - the unredeemed villain, whom everyone identifies right away, and wants to see get his comeuppance. Well aware of the uncomplimentary portrayals of him in my plays, he banned my grandmother and all the household servants from going to shadow theatre performances - though the servants at least managed to evade the ban without getting caught, many times.

No one knows this, but my grandfather and I spoke to each other once. For some reason I can't recall - Angelou's van had broken down, or she was delivering something somewhere - I was making my way to a village nearby on foot for a performance, carrying the suitcase with the figurines, when the Land Rover Hadjimbey had lately taken to going about in, which he drove execrably, screeched to a halt alongside. I would say that we then stared at each other, except that the very dark gold-rimmed sunglasses he wore completely hid his eyes. Let's just say I stared at him, while he faced me. In any event, after a couple of minutes he growled,

- "Get in!"

I obeyed, and he tortured the unfortunate vehicle into first gear. As we sped off, he said, still out of the corner of his mouth,

- "D'you believe all that shit you put in your plays about me?"

I reflected on the question. Did he really think there was a chance that I would say no? And then what? Would he throw his arms around me in a paroxysm of forgiveness? Ask me to come and live with him, take over the farming of his land - implement, with a generation's delay, the surrogate-son plans he had harboured regarding my father? Or would he, Hadjimbey being Hadjimbey, spit in my face, the better to humiliate me for my self-betrayal?

- "Yes," I said.

He turned the sightless greenish-black lenses towards me once more without speaking and stopped the car, leaving the engine running. I climbed out, and he drove off without a backward look. The whole episode had lasted barely five minutes.

That is the sum of my direct experience of my grandfather; but nonetheless, I know a lot about his life and habits, both from my grandmother and from friends I happened to make among the servants. I know, for example, that after Lefki's barrenness had caused Hadjimbey to quit his wife's bed, it became his pleasure to be awakened at sunrise by a servant-girl bringing with her a scalding cup of black coffee, sugared to the consistency of thick syrup to suit his extraordinarily sweet tooth. If the servant-girl happened to be pretty, he would keep her with him for the next hour, sending her off with a pat on the rump when he was ready to get up and properly begin his day. The house, like most others in the village at that time, possessing no bathroom, the arrangements for Hadjimbey's morning ablutions consisted simply of an old-fashioned pitcher and bowl, complemented by a small metal-frame mirror and a cut-throat razor inherited from his father.

As he ran the worn blade raspingly over the recalcitrant stubble, my grandfather would recall his parent, a tailor by trade, who had unwittingly bequeathed to his son a horror of the lot of the small artisan: cooped-up, badly paid, and without any standing in society. Hadjimbey the elder was not, let it be said, a particularly good tailor - the suits he made ran to baggy knees and had lapels that didn't quite sit right. What he excelled at, however, was being completely content with his lot, that is, a low-to-middling social status and little money; and this quality, which he shared with his wife Zinovia, they both utterly failed to transmit to their son, for all that they doted on him. Was it, perhaps, that, as an only child and a son, they doted on him altogether too much? Or was it just chance - the bad seed that the villagers believed in implicitly, and to which they attributed every evil action? Whatever the case, people who knew both the parents and the boy were amazed at how such peaceable, modest people had produced such a monster of ruthless ambition - as though a pair of sheep had somehow brought forth a hyena.

The hyena himself disregarded his mother and father and the example they set almost from birth, resolving very early on to become rich, and important, and have other people work and make a fortune for him. Marriage to a woman with a bountiful dowry was the simple but highly effective expedient by which he began the process of achieving his goals. The mild tailor, on being told of the match, had hesitated before asking, humbly, "Do you love her?" The scornful look which his son gave him silenced him for ever on the subject. At the wedding Hadjimbey's parents sat to one side, for all the world as if ashamed - whether of their son's calculating nature or of their slightly shabby clothes, it was difficult to say.

My grandmother was fond of her in-laws, and visited them regularly in the early days of her marriage; but after Constantia's birth, even though they adored their grandchild, her visits grew rarer, as she began to suspect them too - quite wrongly as it happened - of secretly despising her for her sterility and son-less state. In actual fact they felt sorry for her, and wondered how the proud, egotistical Zenon was taking this unforeseen turn of events. Did he beat her? They wouldn't have been surprised to learn that it was so. But they were intimidated by their son, and never raised the subject with Lefki, so that she in her misery misinterpreted their silence for disapproval and stopped seeing them, except on the occasional saint's day, and at Christmas and

Easter. As for her husband, he would regularly march into his parents' house, growl a curt "Hello - how are you?", and march back out without accepting anything to eat or drink, having deposited a roll of bills on the table, so that they shouldn't disgrace him too much by showing up in church in the same eternal suit and dress every Sunday, or by an excessive plainness in their food and furnishings at home. Out of vanity he also forbade his father from continuing to ply his humble tailor's trade. The old man was too afraid to contravene the ban, and was thus condemned to a weary idleness for the rest of his days. His favourite occupation was to sit on the little porch fronting his house, and watch the passers-by. Once in a while, seeing a former customer walk past, he would murmur to himself, "I made those trousers!" and look longingly after the wearer until he was out of sight. My grandmother was luckier in a way - she still had her cooking and washing and sweeping to sustain her, her son having stopped short of ordering her to acquire a maid. But she, too, pined, in sympathy with her husband. Within ten years of Zenon Hadjimbey's marriage they had both escaped gratefully to the only haven from his egotism left to them: an early grave.

  Poor Lefki was not so lucky. I have said that, after Constantia's birth, Zenon Hadjimbey stopped sleeping with her, and the rest of the time ignored her; but simply to state the fact is hardly to convey the quality of the isolation into which he plunged his helpless victim. He literally never spoke to her again. If he needed to communicate in any way, he would dispatch a message through a servant. At mealtimes, he sat mutely at the head of the table, allowing her to pass him bread, or salt, or dishes of food, but never once looking at her directly.

In the first years, she suffered: she had never loved him, it wasn't that, but she craved the companionship which they had told her any marriage, however unleavened by love, would provide. Had she known that it would come to this hell of loneliness, she would rather have remained a spinster a thousand times. She tried telling her parents, but having finally married her off, they wanted no more of her caprices - told her to go back home and obey her husband, as was her wifely duty. The one or two friends she had among the village women drifted away, as they sensed that their visits were not welcome to the master of the house. But for the servants and her child, Lefki was alone.

She got used to it, in the end, consoling herself with bringing up her daughter and seeing to it that the household was well-run. There was church on Sundays and holy days, and occasionally she would take Constantia to her grandparents' house for a visit. Then, just as the poor woman had resigned herself to living out the rest of her life in this way, Constantia ran off - and it got worse. Lefki had hardly left the sick-bed to which Hadjimbey's beating - itself a sinister, mutely savage affair - had consigned her, when she became aware of unusual activity across the courtyard, where the transfer of some livestock to new quarters had left a barn empty. Not daring to investigate directly, she peered through the window of her room with foreboding, sensing that it all had, in some awful way, to do with her, and dreading the day when she would find out exactly how.

She was not kept in suspense long. Before the week was out, servants marched into her room, and proceeded to transfer her furniture and other belongings to the former barn, cursorily swept out and plastered into rudimentary living quarters. Her husband, she was told, wished her to sleep and eat there now. She was to go over to the main part of the house only if expressly summoned by Hadjimbey. Otherwise the former barn, windowless and still smelling strongly of its previous occupants, was from now on to all intents and purposes her home.

I was sixteen when my grandmother Lefki died, which means that she lived, if it can be called living, in that barn for more than one-and-a-half decades. The clandestine visits she was able to pay my mother kept her alive - Hadjimbey was too busy and too often absent to be able to control her movements absolutely - but they were not enough to keep her sane. I remember her as grotesquely fat, the result of sitting alone in her barn for most of the day, eating marzipan and Turkish delight — let it be granted that at least my grandfather did not starve her - her skin the unhealthy white of prisoners, invalids and other unfortunates who rarely see the light of day, except where it was mottled with the liver spots of age.

Hadjimbey kept the household accounts under far too close a scrutiny for her to be able to give my parents money, but she brought us food, or bolts of material and the like - and once, somehow, a functioning beehive, which my father set on a rising behind the house and which for several years, until the bees caught some sort of disease and died, yielded delicious, thyme-scented honey.

She must have come to our house the year round and at various times of day, but in my memory her visits always seem to take place in winter, at night. I can see the great white whale of her sitting in front of the fireplace, my mother at her side. Her bulky body would rock slightly to a rhythm of its own while she gave little companionable grunts or snuffles; her eyes, more protruding and anxious than ever, would shift from the fire to the hands folded in her lap to my mother to me, in a ceaseless, febrile round. Then suddenly she would bark out,

- "You're not his daughter! And what would he say to that, if he found out!"

Constantia would remonstrate gently: "Mother, come now – don't - ", but Lefki was unstoppable.

- "Yes, yes! Not his! And if he knew with whom!"

And the enormous, insane woman would heave with a silent, malevolent laughter, her mouth yawning, wet and cavernous, but emitting no sound.

- "A son too - a son too! But he doesn't know! And what would he say, if he found out!"

Then, growing conspiratorial,

- "He asked me, the other one - he asked me to marry him."

Here she would grow terrified at her own audacity, and look around, as though fearing to see Hadjimbey looming up behind her out of the shadows. But, the story once launched, she was compelled to finish it.

- "He asked me, yes. He asked me. But I said, 'I can't shame my family's name. No.' He begged! Oh he begged, that other one! I can't tell you! And cried! Like his heart would break! But I said, 'No, don't ask me to shame my family's name. I'll lie with you - have your children - but I'll not shame my husband's name, no.'"

And she would shake her head vehemently, then more and more slowly, her eyes darting from the fire to her hands to my mother, then to me. At that point great tears would begin to roll down her face; then she would sigh, struggle out of her chair, and hobble slowly out of the house, without looking at us again and without saying goodbye.

Her monologues varied in detail, but their themes were constant. Constantia was not Hadjimbey's daughter; she, Lefki, had also borne a son, who was being raised in secret, by the same lover; and this other man, of whom Hadjimbey knew nothing, had often beseeched her to divorce and marry him, continuing to adore her despite her refusal to do so. She never attached a name to this romantic phantom; but it's safe to say that he was the only being, save her daughter, who had ever made her happy.

I have often reflected with amazement on the determination with which my grandfather tortured this innocuous, timid creature. What stock of hatred, what bottomless pool of rage could he have been drawing upon, to be able to maintain such a virulent level of anger towards her for over thirty years? Sometimes, when Angelou and I quarrelled, I would decide that I didn't want to talk to her for a while. In the first hour, it was easy; I was still quite certain that she was wrong, and I right, and wanted nothing to do with her. In the second, an unwelcome little voice would begin to insinuate that, while I was indubitably more right than she was, Angelou might in some respects have a point. By the time three hours were up, I was ready to search her out and apologize for being an ass. Yet what I was unable to keep up for three hours, Hadjimbey had kept up for three decades! It was inconceivable; but he had done it. In a way, it was his life's great achievement - a sort of devil's opus, at its heart not an act of creation but one of destruction. That's why, in my plays, he was a character capable of any evil. Which is what he had meant, presumably, by "all that shit you say about me". Oh yes, I believed it all right.

As for politics, my grandfather was careful to steer well clear of it all. Strictly speaking, the liberation movement presented him with a dilemma. On the one hand, he had no love for the colonial authorities, resenting the heavy and often arbitrary taxes they imposed. On the other, the sort of ethnically-pure state envisioned by the freedom fighters was hardly to his taste. The Moslems represented a far too convenient pool of cheap labour for that; who would cultivate his land and look after his livestock for a pittance, if not they? A more idealistic man might have cast aside such venal considerations and allied himself with the revolutionary movement anyhow, drawn to it despite himself by its slogans of freedom from a foreign yoke. A holy fool might have opposed it, on the grounds that only a revolution which aimed to make all men equal was worth the name, and become a recluse following some gesture on the grand scale, such as giving away all his land to the poor. But Zenon Hadjimbey was neither - he was just a man who wanted the power that goes, not with heroism, either of the active or the passive variety, but with money. So he stayed out of the fray, and waited to see how the dust would settle.

By the time independence came - the hobbled and doomed independence brokered by the country's vengeful colonial masters, at the heart of which Christian-Moslem rivalry lurked like a canker - Zenon Hadjimbey was already in his mid-seventies. Age was no impediment to his ambitions, however. Grossly corpulent and become diabetic from a diet rich in the pastries and sweets which he constantly craved, his lungs half-destroyed by the hand-rolled cigarettes which he smoked from morning till night, his mind remained sharp and the desire for making money still burned inside him bright as ever. And there it was, suddenly spread out before him - the opportunity of a lifetime for quick, easy wealth. Up until then, Hadjimbey had been a rich farmer; that is to say, he put the land he owned to work producing commodities such as wheat, citrus fruit, tobacco, olives and carobs, which he sold at a good profit. Now, almost overnight, he became something quite different: a rich man who need grow nothing, for he already had in hand that most profitable commodity of all: land. Cultivated, lying fallow or completely barren – as long as it was near the sea, it scarcely mattered in a small country which was quickly discovering that its future lay in selling its soul to the devil of tourism. Hadjimbey, who anyway didn't believe in devils, could see the construction rush that was coming; and he knew that for land prices, the sky was going to be the limit.

At the time of my death, he was negotiating his first large sale: an eighteen-donum parcel of prime seaside land, up until then given over to orange and lemon groves. I have no idea of the exact price he was putting on it. But oranges and lemons had become a highly profitable crop; and Hadjimbey, to be sure, had factored this into his targeted profit from the land sale. The bargaining was supposed to be secret, but nothing that goes on in a rich man's house can remain a secret for long when one is a friend of the household servants.

When, therefore, my last play showed Hadjimbey selling the land for thirty pieces of silver, I know reliably that he flew into his most violent rage in a decade. He wasn't the only one selling, it's true - virtually every farmer in the area, big or small, had jumped onto the bandwagon. But none owned as much land as did Hadjimbey and none represented the threat he represented: which was, to my mind at least, no less than the annihilation of our village as we knew it.

And our village is beautiful - with a beauty for whose sake I would have taken on, not merely one Hadjimbey, but one thousand of him and his ilk. I tried to paint it many times: in winter, when the sea at its feet is violet, except where it froths green and white around shoals of rocks; in summer, when the water takes on the blue of dreams, glittering in the sunlight, caressing a bather's skin with soft hands, a sea of pure pleasure, pure joy. I tried to capture the rich umber of the tilled fields, the cool dark green of the citrus groves, the tawny gold of the ripe tobacco, the silver of the olive trees; but there was no way to seize and hold the scent of orange and lemon blossom, of wild thyme and mastic, that filled the salt-tinged air.

How could I fail to oppose Hadjimbey - ready to trade all that glory for a pile of gold, to place it at the mercy of vandals who would tear up the soil, uproot the trees, and in their place raise their hideous cement temples to Mammon? I couldn't really stop him, of course. I was nothing but a manipulator of shadow-puppets, a half-breed, the lowest of the low.

But I wasn't completely without resources: I could at least try to open people's eyes to what was happening in the hope, however slender, that where one person was powerless, many might not be. So I put his dealings in my plays, and showed the desolation that would follow should they come to pass. And he hated me for it.

Chapter Five

It was eight o'clock in the morning, and Ermioni was making her way across the village, bound for Angelou's coffee shop. She walked swiftly, with long strides, her arms swinging at her sides; her right hand gripped the leather satchel containing the paraphernalia of her lay nurse's trade. In contrast to the vigour of her walk, her bony shoulders were hunched, and her brow was knit in a frown. Her hair, braided and coiled around her head in the standard village fashion, was coming loose, but she paid no attention to the renegade strands of brown streaked with grey blowing across her face.

She had been called to Hadjimbey's house an hour earlier; the old man, who was diabetic but ignored the doctor's every dietary injunction, was feeling the effects of a particularly incontinent meal the night before and needed an insulin injection. It was not the first time. Ermioni had packed her satchel with practised speed, and followed the servant who had delivered the message through the cool morning air back to the big house. She found Hadjimbey sitting up in bed, wheezing – against additional doctor's orders, he was also an incorrigibly heavy smoker - and in a foul temper; but Ermioni was not a new maid-servant, to be cowed by glowering looks. She greeted her patient curtly, shot him a brief, sceptical look from beneath slightly raised brows, and without further ado administered the injection.

It was as she made to go, having refastened her satchel, that Hadjimbey spoke up. They were alone in the room; even weakened and gasping by his condition as it was, his voice managed to convey a gleeful malice.

- "Do you know who killed my grandson?"

Ermioni paused beside the door, looking almost haughty. Hadjimbey's wealth and power meant nothing to her; she knew that rich men, too, die.

- "You're asking *me*?"

But Hadjimbey ignored her words, and Ermioni realized that he didn't expect a reply from her. She should have known; important men like Hadjimbey only ever talk to important men like Hadjimbey. And indeed, he answered his own question:

- "He did! Himself! He was too clever for his own good, and it killed him. That's who! Ha, ha!"

The old man's laughter was drowned in a choking cough. From where she stood, Ermioni looked at him with eyes that declared the conversation closed.

- "If you don't feel better by tonight, let me know."

She made to leave, then turned around for a final time.

- "Condolences," she said tartly. She could still hear him coughing and spluttering as she left the house.

Striding towards the women's coffee shop, she puzzled over the conversation in her mind. Was Hadjimbey fishing for information, or did he really know for a fact that his grandson had been murdered? And if he did know, was it Angelou who had told him, or had he found out for himself? The frown was still on her face as she neared the pedlar's house. Despite the early hour the door stood open, the customary signal that the coffee shop was ready to receive patrons. As Ermioni marched over the threshold, she tripped abruptly over the ever-nervous Pulcheria, who had heard her coming and was making good her escape into the street.

- "That fucking cat - "

She heard Angelou's deep-throated laugh from the shadows.

- "She thinks you're the sergeant! 'Morning!"

Ermioni had just managed to save herself from falling, but she continued to fulminate, her eyes having trouble adjusting to the indoor gloom after the brightness of the morning outside.

- "Why don't you open a shutter or two? It's like a cave in here!"

She flung open a window-shutter. Angelou, who was standing at the stove, merely looked on with a smile. She had known Ermioni all her life; she was as familiar with the fey-eyed spinster's sharp tongue and short temper as she was with her own foibles, and equally tolerant of both. Why be otherwise? In Angelou's experience people carried their fundamental nature to the grave.

- "I've just come from the old goat's house."

Ermioni, her rage against Pulcheria spent, sat down at a table and massaged her temples, which were throbbing with the beginnings of a headache. Angelou deposited a cup of sage tea in front of her friend, and pulled up another chair. She was a coffee drinker herself, and called the herbal teas Ermioni swore by, "baby piss". She took a deep draught of scalding black liquid now. No need to ask who the "old goat" was.

- "He's sick?"
- "Ate like a pig again. Needed an injection."
- "Let him croak!"

Ermioni produced a ghost of a smile, then relapsed into her former temple-massaging gloom. There was a pause, while Angelou studied the coffee-grounds in her cup. She didn't really believe in these things, but some women could tell the future... But her mind wasn't on fortune-tellers; she knew Ermioni wanted to say or ask something, and she tried to guess what it might be.

- "He says - "

Ermioni hesitated; Angelou kept very still.

- "He says - somebody killed him."
- "Avraam?"

Ermioni nodded without speaking. Her eyes, to which the muted light from the window lent the greenish-blue of certain sea-pebbles, stared into Angelou's. Angelou held her friend's gaze, returned it.

- "Did he say who?"

- "No. Said his grandson had killed himself, because he was too clever for his boots, some such thing. Being sarcastic."

- "Anything else?"

But Ermioni, resisting Angelou's efforts to turn the tables, shied against further questioning.

- "You tell *me*! What the hell's going on, anyway?"

Ermioni's knobby, spatulate fingers gripped the tea-cup so tightly that Angelou was afraid it would break.

- "Nothing's going on. Hadjimbey's losing his marbles. How old is he anyway? Eighty? Seventy-five?"

- "Never mind him - how old was Avraam Salih? Let's see - three years behind me in school - I was in your class - thirty-six, right? And you're telling me he died, just like that?"

The sound of somebody stepping over the threshold made them both jump. Katerina, her eyes peering through the thick glasses to make out Angelou's companion, recognized Ermioni and beamed.

- "Good morning! Bright and early today, the two of you!"

Ermioni picked up her satchel.

- "I've got to go. I'm doing old Maria today."

- "Poor thing, I'd heard she was on her last legs...she..."

But Ermioni had no wish to become embroiled in a conversation about old Maria's terminal ailments.

Before Katerina had time to finish her sentence, the lay nurse's lanky figure was already half-way out of the door. With a cursory "Later!" tossed over her shoulder, she was gone.

Angelou spent the morning at the coffee shop, talking monosyllabically to the few women who dropped in, doing this and that. She was, for all her air of a woman going about her business as usual, still in shock over Avraam's death; she still half-expected to see her friend walk grinning through the door, ready to own up to a monstrous practical joke. After a brief attempt at a siesta, she gave up and spent the afternoon at the wheel of the blue van, catching up on her pedlar's rounds.

She had taken up peddling as a sideline to the coffee shop-cum-grocery at the end of the 'forties. With the war over for some years now goods were becoming more plentiful, and less expensive. Angelou was able to add household linen and affordable china and cookware to her stock, also ribbons, headscarves and a variety of geegaws. Thereupon she bought a van - sky-blue, her favourite colour - and, to general derision, taught herself to drive. Soon she had acquired clients in all the villages within a half-day's drive from Ayia; everyone knew her, everyone liked her and looked forward to the van's arrival.

When she finally got back home, the sun was going down. As she walked into the house in the failing light, she was overcome by a sense of desolation so strong that it was almost as though a tangible force were pushing her back outside. She opened a tin of corned beef for Pulcheria, filled the cat's water-bowl, and stepped back out into the street, where dusk was rapidly giving way to a starry, moonless night. She would go to Avraam Salih's house; she had to sort out his belongings anyhow, and now was as good a time as any.

It took Angelou a few minutes after opening the dead man's door to register fully the scene that lay before her. The house, lying as it did just beyond the official village limits, lacked electricity, and the torch she was using gave only fragmentary glimpses of the devastation in the room. Swinging its beam spasmodically from place to place she made out one of the walnut wardrobe's two door panels lying on the floor, hacked in pieces, and the other swinging brokenly from dislocated hinges. The wardrobe's contents - a few clothes and a bachelor's supply of bed-linen and towels - were scattered pell-mell around the room; the mattress on Avraam's bed had been ripped apart, and the table and chairs overturned. By its stench, Angelou located a mound of human faeces in one corner; nearby lay a pool of urine. On one wall, daubed crudely in black paint, she made out the slogan: "MOSLEM DOG = SPY"; opposite, the same hand had written: "DEATH TO MOSLEM TRAITORS". She turned around, stepped immediately outside the door, and with a great heave vomited violently onto the ground.

Angelou stayed outside for a long time, squatting on her heels and gulping deep draughts of the night air against the nausea that had overwhelmed her. She looked up, to where the shimmering river of the Milky Way flowed serene and remote above the village. The sight usually enchanted and soothed her, but tonight the rage and disgust inside her were much stronger than its magic. Why? Why? Why? Standing up, she beat her fists against the wall of the house hard enough to draw blood. Why did man derive such pleasure from destroying, violating, defiling? "The only life worth the name, Black Eyes," Avraam used to say, "is lived by those who can create something, where before there was nothing. That's why artists and women are the chosen. You and me, Black Eyes!" To which Angelou would reply, "Chosen to be badly paid and kicked around!" But her retort only fuelled her friend's argument. "That's it! That's why they're badly paid and kicked around! It's God, saying, 'You've been kissed by the Fates - you want to be rich and powerful too? Piss off!'"

Despite the wretchedness of the situation, Angelou found herself laughing out loud at the memory of the conversation. But the laughter died quickly in her throat. If violent death and the even more violent assassination of his memory was the price God had put on Avraam Salih's membership of the chosen, she for one found it too high. And anyway - what God? As she had always remarked acidly to Avraam, "If God made the world, he must have committed suicide soon after." Which remark would make her friend laugh uproariously, but had no impact on his admittedly somewhat eccentric faith in the being he called "The Greatest Shadow Theatre Master of All Time".

Angelou pulled a cigarette out of her shirt pocket, lit it, and tossed the spent match into the darkness. The thought struck her that the unknown vandals might well have finished the job by burning the house down. Why hadn't they? Or had they decided to let people get a good look at their disgusting slogans first, and save that pleasure for their next visit? As the nicotine gradually soothed her jangled nerves, she began to plot her best course of action. It went without question that she would clean up the filth those animals had left behind. Even if they came back to destroy the house the very next day, she wanted them to know that they weren't operating in the total absence of any resistance - that someone existed out there, who was saying "No!". But there was something she had to do before that. Angelou took one last drag on her cigarette and then, stubbing it out with the heel of her sandal, went back inside.

The torch in one hand, she dragged one of the chairs over to the wardrobe and, using it as a step-stool, felt gingerly over the top edge. Grasping something - a handle - firmly, Angelou heaved a large dun-coloured cardboard suitcase with leather-reinforced corners off the wardrobe, letting it down on to the floor with a thud. She stepped hurriedly off the chair and, kneeling down, unfastened the clasps with fingers made clumsy by haste. For a fraction of a second before raising the top she hesitated, as though afraid of what she might see inside. Then, with a decisive movement, she flung it back. In the disc of light from the torch, she peered anxiously at the contents. Miracle of miracles - they hadn't found them! From inside the case, Avraam Salih's shadow theatre figurines presented their calm profiles to her, undisturbed since the last time they had been carefully packed away by their animator, to wait for a performance that never came. Somehow, their survival felt like a victory. Leaving the figurines as they lay, Angelou closed the suitcase and carried it to the van outside. When, about an hour later, she climbed back into the driver's seat and started the engine, it was with a sense of jubilation. "They" might be back; but she felt she had won the day.

Chapter Six

My father used to say: "If you're a worm, you might as well be good at crawling." Meaning that any activity given to one, however humble, was worth doing well. Now, few people probably realize this, but it took a certain amount of talent to be a good shadow-puppet master. Yes, it was unsophisticated entertainment. Yes, it did not even always command, as cinema did from the start, a cash entrance fee, but was often obliged to make do with barter - one egg and a refundable empty shoe-polish jar per adult, three buttons per child, in the pre-war years. Nonetheless, it required sufficient imagination to invent several new plots each year; in addition one had to possess sufficient artistry not only to manipulate the figurines convincingly, but also to manufacture them in the first place out of the classic child's materials of cardboard, glue and paint. Then there was the singing, for a performance was not a performance without songs, and not having a voice was a serious handicap; plus, it was useful to be able to play at least a rudimentary accompanying instrument. One was obliged, as well, to act as one's own impresario, mapping out an annual itinerary and schedule of performances, haggling with coffee shop keepers over the rental of space, working out transport from venue to venue.

Thereby, as long as rival entertainments such as cinema and television had not yet terminally eroded the audience, one earned enough to feed and clothe oneself, and maintain the shadow-figurines and few props in good trim. As for reputation, one either became known as a good shadow theatre master or one did not, but that had no bearing on earnings. As long as the audience existed, it was a captive one, starved of spectacle and flocking indiscriminately to whatever was on offer; they might applaud a good performance more loudly, but they would sit through a bad one just the same. By the same token, by the time of my death not even the best shadow theatre - and mine, false modesty aside, was a good contender for the title - could manage to pay its way, let alone turn a profit.

The effervescent young man from the state television station who showed up one fine day, intoning "cultural deracination" and "the spontaneity of folk-art" and I don't know what else - I didn't spell it out for him: that by now I was lucky if I managed to stage one or two performances a year, that I was reduced to working as a day-labourer for the Public Works Department digging ditches and repairing roads for a living. But I did try to explain that the shadow theatre was finished, like a person who had reached the end of his life-span, and that, just as with a dying person, one couldn't put the clock back or gainsay nature; the most one could hope for, in my humble view, was that there might be something left behind for the heirs. That's to say, that some elements of the shadow theatre might survive and be propagated in, for instance, cartoons, or even painting.

He brushed it all aside, however - wouldn't even listen, convinced that just because one twenty-seven-year-old TV producer had found out there was such a thing as shadow theatre and was about to make a programme showing off about it, this was going to bring about a renaissance of the genre, no less. That's what he said: "There's going to be a real renaissance of the genre, my friend, mark my words! A renaissance of the genre!" before speeding off in the snazzy red sports car bought to impress the girl television employees. I pictured him listening to American music on his newly-acquired record-player and drinking imported whiskey, the price of one bottle of which would have kept me and the shadow theatre going for a month, as he dreamed of taking one of those new female programme announcers, all peroxide hair and imitation-Hollywood make-up, to bed; and I thought to myself that "cultural deracination" had some strange opponents.

Why had he chosen me? After all, there were still two or three other shadow theatre masters out there struggling to survive, all much older and more experienced than I was; one in particular, Odysseas Kamenos, who had been my teacher, was universally rated a genius, with a repertoire of dozens of plays of his own devising, and hundreds of figurines, to his name.

Patiently, he explained it all to me in his self-important little way: that I had been chosen precisely because he wanted to show that the shadow theatre was not, as everyone thought, *passé* in line with the wildly-coloured syrupy drinks we'd all had to make do with before Coca-Cola, but still a vibrant, young art form - those were his words: "vibrant, young art form" - with a future. He was too polite, or perhaps too sly, to refer to my mixed origins. Perhaps he intended to gloss over them entirely? Or, on the contrary, to dress them up as proof of the government's rather nervous case that all was well between the country's Christians and Moslems? Maybe he would even be rash enough to present me as a walking, talking example of an art form common to, and enriched by the intermingling of, the two cultures - one never knew with these young, ambitious types.

In any event, I wasn't altogether unhappy with the prospect of his film. In fact, I went to work right away on the short play he wanted to include in it. The village, of course, was all agog with the news: "A man from the television came, and Avraam Salih's going to be a film star!"

Even Angelou teased me,

- "Now that you're going to be famous you won't want to go around in a pedlar's van any more, will you, Mister Cary Grant!"

But I couldn't bear her joking about that, and would always cut her short.

- "You know I'll never leave you, Black Eyes; now just shut up."

Which only made her laugh all the harder; but I could sense the relief in her, as palpable as that of a stray dog which realizes you've decided to take it home with you.

    I fell in love with Angelou one sweet spring day, in my twenties. I was walking to a performance, carrying the suitcase with the props and figurines; the fields and the roadside were lush with a profusion of asphodels, marguerites and wild orchids, the sky a fresh clear blue, and when I heard a car approaching behind me I was irritated, thinking it ruined everything with its stink and noise. When it pulled up alongside I kept on walking without turning my head, as though if I refused to pay attention to it, it might return the favour and disappear. Then a voice made of honey and woodsmoke said,
    - "Avraam Salih!"
and I couldn't look away any longer.

    I knew it was Angelou; there was no mistaking that voice. As I started to climb into the van through the door she had swung open for me, I felt suddenly amazed that what was happening now had not happened sooner. As a small boy at the village elementary school I had had a crush on Angelou; but she was three years older than I, and treated me, if she noticed me at all, with a motherly condescension which reduced my adoration to nothing but a small child's game. Then she finished school and I forgot about her; saw her about the village doing this or that, to be sure, but remotely, as one looks at a stranger or the figure of a person - man? woman? - busy at something very far away. Now, suddenly, the opposite had happened; by materializing unexpectedly as she had on that deserted road, beneath that crystalline, unblemished sky, Angelou was suddenly thrust to the forefront, as it were, of my life; and I looked at her with the sweet, relieved astonishment one feels at suddenly noticing, after one has been in and out of a room several times, that a key one has been missing anxiously for days is in fact lying on the table, and must have been there all the time.

- "Where are you going?"
- "Dev Kebir. For a show."
- "Thought so."

She was wearing trousers of some rough dark blue stuff and a man's white shirt open at the throat; her hair, unbraided, lay coiled loosely on the nape of her neck. She looked, for those parts, like no other woman alive. Which is just how she struck everyone else too; one reason the village was so philosophical about her was that she was considered too *sui generis* to set a dangerous example for wives and daughters.

- "What are you staring at? Never seen a woman driving before, right?"

That was the least of it; but for that matter, she knew full well I hadn't.

- "Right."
- "Stare away then. I'm a good driver. You might learn something."
- "No use. I'm too scared to drive."

Her peals of laughter filled the van.

- "Scared? And why?"
- "Too fast, cars. I like things slow."

Her face was deadpan, but the black eyes were wicked.

- "Slow has its advantages."

I wanted to kiss her. I wanted to show her what I meant by slow. But, indefinably, she shut me off. For the rest of the way we said nothing.

At the Dev Kebir coffee shop she stopped the van.

- "Thanks, Angelou."
- "It was nothing. Goodbye."

She was off without a look. I hoisted the suitcase, and walked inside.

The show that day was a love story, standard fare. A rich man's son falls in love with a poor girl; but he wants her to love him for himself, not for his money. So he pretends to be a labourer, and woos her. His friend, Karagöz, is the comic relief; he's in on the subterfuge but can't keep a secret, and is forever on the brink of giving the game hilariously away. Since there always has to be a villain, I put in the Hadjimbey character in the guise of a second rich man, a merchant, who also wants the girl; he knows she loves somebody else, so he's getting ready to kidnap her. But Karagöz gets wind of the plan, tells his friend, and the girl is saved in the most agreeable way. On their wedding-day the groom reveals his real identity to the bride, and they live happily ever after. Predictable? I'd be the first to say so. But masterpieces, you'll admit, have been composed around plots hardly less slight. Not that I'm claiming masterpiece status for the show in question;

just saying the quality of the figurines - I always kept the forms simple: the essence of a beautiful girl, the essence of a handsome lover - and a certain amount of wit in the dialogue may have struck the lightest of taps for posterity that day.

I didn't think about Angelou again until it was over, the suitcase packed, the coffee shop keeper paid. Then I looked up and there she was at the door, conjured up as needed for the second time that day.

- "If you want a ride back, I'm going that way."

I wanted a ride back. This time the silence was companionable. Outside my house, she said,

- "I go around the villages. So do you. Makes sense to go together."

- "Can't pay you much, Angelou."

- "Pay me what you pay the bus. You don't always walk, do you?"

- "No. Just lucky today."

She looked at me, gravely, then started up the engine. I wished I hadn't said it, tried in embarrassment to move the conversation along.

- "Where next, then?"

- "Kapnou. Saturday."

- "I'll see what I can set up. In any case, the next time you're going my way."

- "The next time I'm going your way."

She raised her hand in both agreement and farewell. I stood and watched the van drive off, a dwindling object of sky-blue in the dying light of day.

On Saturday - I had decided to take a chance on Kapnou, just show up and see what kind of crowd I could muster - I walked to the women's coffee shop a little after lunch. Through the open door I heard female voices, Angelou's laughter. In a voice still laced with drollery, I heard her call out,
- "Come in!"

I had never been there before. Confusedly, I took in the tables and chairs, the big four-poster against the far wall, the shelves crammed with household odds and ends, the fire-place and cooking stove. At one of the tables sat Angelou and Ermioni, lingering amusement on both their faces, cups of coffee and a bottle of brandy before them. The nurse's eyes, more grey than blue today, stared directly into mine. I looked at Angelou, who slapped her hand on the table as though to mark the end of the two women's conversation, and stood up, stretching.
- "All right then. Ermioni, it's time."

Ermioni pulled back her chair, put a hand up to her forehead.
- "God. I've got a headache. I knew I shouldn't've had that coffee."

She grimaced. Angelou grinned.
- "Oh, come on. You can't drink that baby piss all day. Anyway, coffee's good for headaches."

The nurse, with the resigned air of someone who has heard it all before, stood up in turn.
- "You stick to your poison and I'll stick to mine. See you later."

She flashed me another look, waved a vague salute to Angelou, and stepped outside. The image of a woman on a bicycle was framed in the doorway for an instant; then it vanished.

Angelou was gathering up the cups. Today her trousers were khaki; through the loose man's shirt, I could make out the movement of her breasts. I pictured her naked, with her black hair loose.

- "What time's the show?"
- "Six."
- "All right. We'll go to Kamares and Eleou first. It's early enough."

I had decided against a love story that day, in favour of adventure. Alexander the Great, equipped with sword, magnificent steed, and a lot of poetic license, slays the dragon, finds the answer to riddles posed by the Sphinx, captures Xerxes, and frees a beautiful princess from slavery with hardly a pause. Karagöz, once again, is cast for laughs: the faithful servant clever in his utter stupidity, without whose help not even the magnificent Alexander could have carried the day. Moral (noticed by not a single person save the puppet-master): there's always some insignificant little man doing his anonymous heroic best behind the achievements of the great. Anyhow, the audience enjoyed it; and if they chose to identify with Alexander rather than Karagöz, with the master rather than the slave, who was I to set them straight?

Back in Ayia, I said to Angelou,

- "I'll walk from here. You don't have to drive all the way to my place."
- "Come and have something to eat first. I cooked this morning. It's ready."

It occurred to me then that organization is where women's superiority over men lay. What had I done before going over to the women's coffee shop? Struggled awake, had some bread and a coffee over yesterday's newspaper, fed Pulcheria's predecessor, and then walked out with the suitcase, leaving the dishes still in the sink, the cat's plate on the floor, and the bed unmade. It didn't even occur to me to think that by the time I got home it would be dinner-time, and therefore what would there be to eat, and so forth. But Angelou! By what I had seen at her house, the bedclothes were smooth, the floor swept, there was no dust on the furniture nor any ashes in the grate; she had had time for coffee and a gossip with a friend; and, it now transpired, she had made supper in advance, and it stood waiting to be served - no last-minute rummaging for odds and ends in the larder, no wait. It was magnificent in its everyday way.

Back in the coffee shop she busied herself with the food, began to lay the table.
- "It's just potato and beet salad, and salted herring. D'you like it?"

I liked potato and beet salad. And salted herring. I would have eaten dog scraps just to be allowed to stay.

When we had finished, she refilled our glasses with wine and leaned back in her chair, eyes half-closed. Tentatively, I said,
- "Angelou?"
- "Yes?"
- "Don't you care?"
- "What about?"
- "The village. What they'll say."

She smiled and shrugged, a slight, bitter twist to her lips.
- "As though they don't have better things to do!"

She saw the look on my face. There were question marks in her eyes.
- "You remind me of my mother. She had a bad labour when I was born. They told her God was punishing her for marrying a Turk, and she said just what you said. 'As though He doesn't have better things to do!'"

Angelou laughed.
- "I remember your mother. She smelled of rose-water in church. I used to try and stand next to her. You look alike, in a way." She glanced at me, as if assessing the accuracy of her own remarks, then away. "Better than I remember my own mother, really."

As I was about to speak, she got up and began to clear the dishes. I held back the words. Instead, I said again,
- "Don't you care?"

She laughed, louder this time.

- "Let them refuse me for a daughter-in-law! I don't want their sons anyhow!"

I said, my heart in my mouth,

- "D'you want me?"

She stood stock still, not looking at me.

- "Not that way."

I persisted. Something had happened to my heart, which felt swollen to twice its usual size.

- "What way, then?"

Slowly, she sat back down.

- "Listen, Avraam. I like you. Your father sent you to that fancy school in town so you could go and study and become a big-shot, but you came back here and set up the shadow theatre and go around making shillings and piastres because that's your way. I know what's going on, I've watched you. You're half-Turk, in a Christian village; your grandfather is rich and mean and he hates you; and you're all alone like me, no mother or brother or father. If I don't help you, who will? But - "

She paused. I could see that she was struggling to find the right words. I waited, hardly breathing. I wanted to die.

- "But I'm not - men don't - I can't love men. If I could, I'd love you, I think. But I can't do it."

Her voice was wavering, humble. I saw that her eyes were filled with tears. She was crying because of me! I was desperate. I no longer cared about my own misery; I just wanted her to be happy. I said, panic-stricken,

- "Angelou, stop. Stop! I love you. You know I love you. But I won't talk about it - you musn't cry about it. I won't talk about it! I promise!"

The tears didn't fall, receded. She managed a small smile. I felt insubstantial, like the ghost of myself. In some way, it seemed, I had indeed died. I said, my voice sounding remote to my own ears,
- "Agreed? I'll ride with you?"
- "I'll paint the van tomorrow."
We shook hands. Hers was ice-cold.
- "I'll help you. What time?"
- "Noon or so. I'll drive it over to your house."
And that's how the sign on the van came about.

Chapter Seven

It was August the fifteenth, the feast of the Assumption of the Virgin. Angelou woke up early, braided and pinned up her hair, and donned what she thought of as her church uniform: a wine-red dress cut simply, its sole adornment a small lace collar at the throat, and on her feet, instead of the usual men's shoes or sandals, a pair of low-heeled pumps in conscientiously-polished black leather. A handbag being, even now, too much for her, she instead tucked a neatly-folded handkerchief into one sleeve cuff and slipped a few coins for the collection box into a concealed pocket. She was ready.

Angelou went to church for two reasons. First, she was by nature gregarious and drew warmth from the communal life of the village in all its manifestations; and second, she loved the Byzantine chanting which accompanied the service. The right-hand cantor, in particular, was a fine baritone; and when the full, sweet notes expanded and rose above the incense and the burning candles to reach the vaulted ceiling, Angelou felt her heart and spirit surge with it.

She, too, had a beautiful singing voice, mellow and effortless; but the role of cantor being reserved for men only, Angelou had to content herself with singing popular songs at christenings or weddings. This she did

gladly, and was in great demand for such occasions. Avraam Salih used to tease her, and say,
- "Sophia Vembo herself!"
naming a Greek singer whose voice dominated the airwaves of the day. And it was true: at the right time and in the right place Angelou also might have become rich and famous by simply doing what she did best and loved doing the most. She rarely thought about it, but when she did, it seemed to her that to gain recognition for a true talent must be the most benignly-starred of fates; but it wasn't to be her own.

She thought about it now, as she walked to the church through the clear morning air, which already held a promise of the high heat to come: the forecast was for over a hundred degrees in the shade. Somewhere at the back of her mind she resolved to go down to the watermelon patch later - it would be cooler near the sea. But what preoccupied her was not really singing, or the weather. She recalled Avraam Salih's house as she had seen it the night before, soiled and half-destroyed; she saw Avraam himself laid out, dead, on his poor bed, and then she saw the empty grave. The sense of desolation which had led her to the house the previous evening swept over her again.

By now she had reached the church; stepping inside, the familiar rituals of lighting a candle and kissing the icon consoled her temporarily. For the rest of the service she let her mind drift; to an outside observer she seemed absorbed in the liturgy, quiet and passive. But in her mind, she was wary and alert. Something – she sensed it - was going to happen.

The service was over; but everyone stayed in their places, expectant. Somewhere in the men's section of the church there was a stirring; in a minute or two this resolved itself into a parting of the ranks of the congregation, stiff in their best clothes, to allow someone who had been standing among them to pass through to the pulpit. The women whispered it among themselves: it was a preacher, a theologian, who had never been to the village before, dispatched specially by the bishop. As this personage climbed the ornate spiral staircase and emerged over the pulpit rail the villagers took in his appearance: on the short side, a little plump, with thinning reddish hair, a complexion to match, and eyes of a muddy brown which, behind wire-rimmed spectacles, were wide with what was presumed to be religious fervour.

Amid a chorus of noses being blown, coughs being coughed, and the restive sounds of bored children, the theologian sent by the bishop unfolded a piece of paper and began to declaim. As far as it went, it was standard fare. Having determined after a few sentences that it was so, those listening set their mental gears to neutral and began to think about the feasting to come, which every year on this day involved roasting a goat or sheep on a spit and making merry in the open air.

But suddenly something, a slight change, a gathering urgency, in the theologian's tone, brought them back to the church and the immediate present, and they began to pay attention. The red-haired preacher, eyes more fervent than ever, had just finished asking the Lord to protect the country, the country's President, and the country's valiant Armed Forces. Normally, that would have been the end of the sermon; it would remain only for everyone to cross themselves, take communion, and go home. But this sermon, clearly, was going to be different. The theologian put aside his paper; but he was not finished. He waited theatrically, let the premature shuffling of feet subside, then said,

- "In addition, my attention has been drawn to a particular incident by His Grace the Bishop. I understand that a few days ago the death occurred, under mysterious circumstances, of an inhabitant of this village."

There was a febrile stirring and murmuring in the crowd. The women crossed themselves; the men pulled out handkerchiefs and mopped their brows. Everyone's eyes had involuntarily turned to one spot: the varnished olive-wood pew where Zenon Hadjimbey sat, bald dome gleaming, apparently slumbering through the service. He did not move now; but those nearest to him could discern that his eyes under their heavy lids were in fact half-open, like those of a lizard lying in wait for its prey.

The preacher was warming to his task. Raising his arms up, he said, in a louder voice,

- "I shall not go into details. I shall not recall shameful events, name names best left unmentioned. But I shall say this: Christian shall cleave to Christian; believer, to believer. Where this law is violated, only evil can result. Only evil, I say! This man who died - this offspring of sin - "

But the rest of his words were drowned out by Angelou's terrific roar of rage. Breaking away from the body of women, arms flailing, she charged at the staircase leading to the pulpit, tried to wrest it from its support with her bare arms.

- "You tomato-faced abomination! You excuse for a man! You come down here and I'll show you sin!"

She was screaming, her face contorted with rage. The preacher, peering over the rail, had grown very pale.

- "You come in here and bad-mouth the dead! You're not worth Avraam Salih's little finger! You abortion! You scum! Devil!"

By now the priest and sacristan had collected themselves and, rushing to where Angelou was now threatening to climb the stairs, seized her arms on either side and half-pushed, half-marched her out of the church. As they went, the sacristan was trying to calm the maenad:

- "Now Miss Angelou - it's not so bad - now Miss Angelou, calm yourself - "

But Angelou was not to be appeased. Once outside, she shook off the two men's hold, turned on them angrily:

- "And you lot just stand there, listening to that rubbish! Saying nothing! Doing nothing! You should be ashamed! 'Offspring of sin', and I don't know what rubbish!"

She stopped, wiped some spittle from one corner of her mouth with her sleeve, and walked off without looking at the two men, shaking her head. The priest and the sacristan watched her for a moment; then, the face of each averted from the other, they went back inside. Throughout the church, chaos reigned; the theologian, brow glistening with sweat, was being helped down from the pulpit, children dashed around with excited whoops, and both men and women stood gossiping openly. It took half an hour to calm everyone down sufficiently for communion, and for the priest to wind up the service with a modicum of dignity. By then neither the preacher nor Zenon Hadjimbey were anywhere in sight.

When Angelou got home, she was still trembling with a ferment of emotion in which sorrow argued and wrestled with anger. Sorrow for Avraam Salih; for herself; but also, somehow, for the entire village, the sacristan, the priest - even the theologian sent by the bishop, all of whom she felt had acquiesced to something shameful and base. Everyone was diminished, somehow less than they had been before that morning's service. Pulcheria, curled sleeping on a wicker chair, raised her head and fixed Angelou for a moment with her green gaze; then, perceiving there was nothing she could do, covered her face with her paws and became a rhythmically breathing heap of grey fur again. Her new owner poured herself a shot of brandy, drank it down. Then she threw off the church costume, put on trousers, shirt and sandals again, gathered together a bottle of wine, a piece of cheese from the larder, and half a loaf of bread wrapped in a chequered napkin, and made for the door. At the sound of the van's engine revving up, Pulcheria, without moving, gave her characteristic brief, raucous meow, and settled down to continue her siesta.

By the time Angelou had reached the watermelon patch it was noon, and the whole landscape was ablaze. The sea, a blue promise of relief from the oven-like heat, lay a short walk away, at the end of the eucalyptus-lined road; she could see and smell it. The patch was big enough to accommodate a couple of dozen watermelon plants, among which the fruit lay strewn on the ground like so many dark green footballs; and, to one side, a three-sided shelter of woven straw and cane shading a ramshackle camp-bed and a wooden table covered with patterned oilcloth. The only other structure was a stone well standing in the middle of the patch; rigged to its rim was a rusty pump to which was connected a bright yellow hose.

Angelou, emerging from the van, deposited the bread, cheese and wine on the table, then made for the pump and pulled the starter cord, releasing a shuddering thump - thump - thump and the sound of gushing water into the still air. Two or three fields away she could see smoke rising and make out tiny figures milling around its source; a family group was making ready to celebrate Assumption Day. This was the first time Angelou was spending the holiday alone. Avraam Salih's death had, apparently, thrown everyone off, and for once neither Liza, nor Ermioni, nor any other of the coffee shop's patrons had thought to invite its keeper, as they usually did, to spend the day with them, drinking and singing. Avraam, though invited too, usually stayed away; he was shy, and disliked large groups of people as much as Angelou revelled in them. If she pressed him, saying people would take offense, and that anyway they would like to hear him sing some songs from the shadow theatre plays, he became angry and fretful.

- "Go, go, for God's sake! I don't like it, all right?"

And Angelou, sighing a martyr's sigh, would go alone. She wanted him to come not because she really thought people would be offended but because she was at her best on this kind of occasion, joking, laughing, vivid; and when she sang - everyone always begged her to sing to round off the feasting - her voice was warm and strong and true, marvellous to hear. It was vanity, and a slightly cruel vanity at that, but she wanted Avraam to hear her, to see her on such a day; she wanted to make him love her even more than he did already. She didn't love him sexually; but she loved him enough to be afraid that without sex she would lose him. Her singing was a substitute, the bait of a fisherman who doesn't have the right bait. But each time, when she got home after dark, having been away all day, and Avraam stood up smiling from his book or newspaper to meet her, Angelou was ashamed of her motives, and almost winced at the passion in his eyes. He never talked about it, never tried to force the situation; it seemed to be enough for him that she needed him to adore her.

Angelou, having made sure the water was flowing freely among the watermelons, went to the shelter and lay down on the camp-bed. Behind her closed eyelids images of the morning's happenings flashed in a restless succession. She felt dismayed at the spectacle she had made of herself; but she also felt proud. She couldn't have let the preacher's slander go unanswered! And if she hadn't spoken up, no one else would have dared to do it. Never mind that a good number among the congregation were undoubtedly thinking the sermon was stuff and nonsense. She, more than anyone, knew the collective spirit of the village: it was tolerant, not out of any superior knowledge or sophistication, but because it was prosaic. Being so, it was not easy prey to idealistic propaganda. The theologian sent by the bishop might rant on about the evils of miscegenation, but all the village had seen in Avraam Salih during the thirty-six years of his life was a quiet young man who, far from causing anyone trouble, gave everybody pleasure with his shadow theatre. Let anyone who wanted call him an offspring of evil; the village just did not, and would not, see it that way.

It was the same with Angelou herself; another community might well have looked askance upon a woman who wore trousers, drove a car and ran a women's coffee shop - but as the village of Ayia saw it, it caused no harm, so why be bothered? The theoretical ramifications of it all did not enter people's minds. If someone tried to make an issue of it, they themselves would be seen as a trouble-maker, rather than the person they were attempting to denounce.

What would Avraam himself have thought of what was going on? The thought brought a wry smile to Angelou's lips. He'd have approved of the spirit of her actions; but the actions themselves would have appalled him. Making a lot of noise in public wasn't his way - meetings, political rallies, speeches, committees, were as alien to him as cat's fur to a dog. Avraam was a rebel, but he staged his rebellions alone, elaborating them in private and expressing them only through his plays. He made wonderful plays...told wonderful stories...

On the brink of sleep now, Angelou began to recall Avraam's favourite tale about watermelons: Nasreddin Hodja is taking a walk and sees a watermelon patch by the road, full of enormous fruit lying on the ground. A little further along he comes upon an oak tree laden with acorns and sits down to rest in its shade, thinking: "Truly, Allah sometimes disposes of things in a peculiar way: here is this enormous tree with such tiny fruit upon it, while a humble watermelon plant which can't even raise itself off the ground bears fruit as huge as cannon-balls." The Hodja falls asleep; then an acorn drops on his pate and startles him awake. Whereupon he shakes his head and says: "Allah, I see your point!"

Almost detached by now from the outside world, Angelou sensed, rather than heard, a car approaching; between half-closed eyelids she saw a black Morris Oxford pull up and stop in the shade of a eucalyptus with a protesting screech of its brakes. For a moment nothing moved; then the door on the driver's side opened and a man in a short-sleeved white shirt, striped tie and trousers as black as the body of the Morris stepped out. He looked about him; then, spotting Angelou in the hut's shade, he set his face in a broad smile and began to walk towards her.

Angelou, pretending to be asleep, lay tensed against the moment when he would reach her. She didn't know the man, but she didn't have to; he represented, she knew intuitively, more trouble. The only question was, of what kind. He was at the hut; he stopped a few feet from her. He cleared his throat.

- "Miss Angelou?"

He spoke the Greek dialect, but by his accent she knew he was a Moslem. With a mental sigh of resignation she opened her eyes, feigned surprise.

- "What? Oh!"

She sat up.

- "Sorry, I was asleep. Who are you looking for?"

The man's smile was as broad as ever. His face was round, with affable dimples; his teeth were white and even.

- "Excuse me, Miss Angelou. Osman, journalist. At your service."
- "Yes?"

Angelou scrutinized the small white card he had conjured up out of a pocket. The man cleared his throat again. The dust of the journey, perhaps, was giving him some trouble. Angelou, despite herself, felt moved to get up and pour some water into a tin cup from an earthenware jug set at the foot of the camp-bed.

- "Your health. I don't have coffee here, excuse me."

He drank deeply.
- "Your health!"

Then, as though feeling some small talk were necessary,
- "We're burning up! The radio said one hundred and three in the shade to day!"

Angelou clicked her tongue impatiently.
- "Well, Mr. Osman?"

He handed the cup back to her, looked at her directly.
- "I want to talk to you. About the case of Mr. Avraam Salih."

Angelou frowned, but made no answer. She waited.
- "My newspaper is very interested, you see. He was a Moslem in a Christian village...we heard...ahem...we heard he was murdered...his house vandalized..."

Angelou's eyes flashed.

- "His mother was a Christian. And who told you all this, anyhow?"

The journalist gazed at her with a slight smile. He said nothing. Angelou crossed her arms.

- "It seems to be the day for you lot today!"

He looked intrigued; and she realized that of course he couldn't know about the theologian sent by the bishop. Well, she wouldn't be the one to enlighten him. She said,

- "What do you want, anyway?"

The man switched off his smile, judging it unsuitable for getting down to business.

- "My newspaper will pay one hundred pounds" - he paused for effect - "for an interview about Avraam Salih's life, and photographs of the house. I have my photographer here; everything is ready, he could take them now." He gestured towards the car where, for the first time, Angelou made out a second man in the rear. She felt a slight shock, as though more men, an invisible army, might be hidden round about. The thread of unreasonable fear that shot through her lent as extra edge to her anger.

- "Go to the devil! Get out! Out! Out!"

For the moment, Osman stood his ground.

- "One hundred and fifty pounds!"

He began to pull a wad of banknotes from trouser-pocket. Angelou, striding across the hut, picked up a hoe propped up against one wall and advanced towards the journalist. As she raised the tool aloft, he held up one hand in a reciprocal gesture.

- "All right, Miss Angelou! All right!"

Then, seeing that she was still walking towards him with the hoe, he turned tail and walked rapidly back to the Morris. In a moment the car moved off, towards the sea; Angelou waited for the sound of it reversing direction, then watched the black carapace reappear, pass the watermelon patch once again, and move out of sight. Its driver did not look at her as the car went by. Through the rolled-down window, the photographer in the back directed the camera's eye at Angelou. Whether the shutter had clicked or not, there was no way for her to know.

Angelou waited until the sound of the car's engine had faded; then, with a somnambulist's bearing, she set down the hoe, walked towards the well and switched off the pump. As she did so, the absurd thought crossed her mind that she would tell Avraam all about this when she got home. There was a silence lasting a fraction of a second before the frenetic whirr of the cicadas, obscured until now by the noise of the machine, reclaimed the blazing midday air; simultaneously, Angelou slumped to her knees. Arms resting on the well's rim, she finally began to weep the tears - primeval, violent - she had not yet wept over Avraam Salih's death. She stayed there, racked by sobs so wrenching they sounded scarcely human, for a long time. But no one heard her, and no one came.

Chapter Eight

The caption under the photograph in the next day's edition of the newspaper "Hakikat" read: "Angelou Pieri, mistress of the murdered man, threatening our reporter". It pictured a blurry Angelou, hair dishevelled, staring straight at the camera while grimly clutching her hoe. In the accompanying article, "our Special Correspondent", unnamed, described how, during his visit to the village of Ayia to investigate reports of the savage slaying a few days earlier of A. Salih, the sole resident Moslem, he and the newspaper's photographer received a universally hostile reception, culminating in an armed assault by Angelou Pieri, pedlar, described by sources who did not wish to be identified as the dead man's mistress. According to the same sources the evidence pointed to a political killing, motivated by the ethnic hatreds which render peaceful coexistence impossible between the Moslem and Christian communities; following the murder, Salih's house was known to have been looted and vandalized, the perpetrators in addition daubing on the walls the slogans: "Moslem Dog = Spy" and "Death To Moslem Traitors". The article ended with the rhetorical question, in bold type: "How long must our people live in fear of their lives?"

The article also described me as "an entertainer, known for his quiet and harmless character". Well, "harmless" is a big word; and I'll admit that it gave me a pang of conscience, juxtaposed as it was with all that stuff about "the dead man's mistress". Our special correspondent got the slogans on the walls of my house right; but as for who was or wasn't my mistress, he hadn't a clue, nor did he care. This had to be a political slaying, or for his purposes it was nothing.

Angelou and I.....no correspondent, however special, could have understood how it was with us. In literature, love-stricken young men who cannot for one reason or another attain the true object of their desires usually turn to a life of restless dalliance, abandoning one light, unsatisfying liaison for the next in a doomed and ceaseless round. Sometimes they manage to exit the cycle and achieve emotional nirvana thanks to a change of heart, an eleventh-hour yielding on the part of *the* lady in their lives; sometimes their escape is a tragic one, through bullet-in-the-temple-type suicide or elective death in some glorious far-flung battle. Only very rarely do they settle down to a monogamous affair with another woman whom they do not love and whom, had *the* lady been available, they would not have looked at twice. This is what happened to me.

Why? You might well ask, and so do I. Judging by the looks the girls and women gave me at shadow theatre performances, I was attractive enough to the opposite sex to render restless dalliance a serious option; and my own father's prehistory provided both inspiration and example. If I didn't follow in his footsteps, it was thanks neither to prudishness nor prudence - I was, it seems to me, conspicuously lacking in either. It was, rather, a case of a curious abeyance of the self, a nervous, involuntary inversion of perception, which, as soon as I had set my sights on an attractive victim, immediately placed me in the victim's shoes, instantly making impossible either word or action. I felt the eager female heart beating in the breast, the awakening love, the desire; and experienced, as vividly as though I myself were the victim, the inevitable tears and anguish over the abandonment to come, the bitter realization that when it comes to love, any man, however trustworthy in all other respects, can lie. It was like deliberately running over small game in the road: some people could do it - went out of their way to make it happen; but I, though I liked hare stewed in wine well enough, couldn't.

So there I was, likely game myself - dying with desire for a woman who wouldn't have me, and unable to chase skirts to relieve the burden. To any woman with eyes in her head and half a brain, it was obvious that I could be had for the taking. The one who reached out to take was Ermioni; and she had me.

It happened one early morning in March. Angelou and I had been peddling our wares, she literally and I figuratively, around the villages of the district for almost a year now, and the van with its dual sign was by now a well-established sight. If there was gossip about it, and there must have been some, it didn't in any way affect our lives.

It had rained the night before, an invigorating, spring rainfall; but now the sun was out, and I was sitting in the front yard half-asleep, basking in its warmth, when Ermioni materialized on the road that ran past the house, approaching from the direction of the bridge with her lanky stride.

- "Got a shovel?"

This was classic Ermioni. In the village she was already famous for her curtness; and the chances of getting a civil "how are you" from her were rated as slim as those of her ever making a good marriage.

- "Good morning!"

My tone was, I hoped, ironic. She gave me a look.

- "I killed a snake back there. Got a shovel?"

My peaceful doze in the sun seemed to be at an end. I sighed, stood up, went into the house and through to the back, found the shovel, brought it back out to her. She took it and marched off the way she had come, not looking to see whether or not I followed. When we got to the little bridge I saw the dead snake lying in the middle of the road, its head crushed by a rock. It was squat and thick as a man's arm, with bright triangular markings; the most poisonous kind. Ermioni rolled the rock to one side with her foot, manoeuvred the snake onto the shovel blade, and tossed it over the parapet of the bridge into the undergrowth below.

- "What were you doing over here?"

I expected her to tell me to mind my own business, but her reply was prompt.
- "Gathering snails."

The weather was right for it, and the season; but she was carrying neither bag nor basket. There was a silence. Her eyes, neither one colour nor another, mocked me. For the first time I noticed the green in their depths, and how it sometimes dominated their grey-blue in a certain mood or quality of light. I said, lamely,
- "Want a coffee?"
- "No - no thanks."

The first refusal was standard village good manners. Even though this was Ermioni, I allowed for it, asked her again. She looked uncharacteristically demure.
- "I don't mind."

She was still on her best behaviour when we got to the house, waiting to be asked before sitting down, wishing me a polite "Your health" before taking her first sip of coffee. I was awkward, forgetting to offer her a glass of water, spilling my own coffee into the saucer. When she had finished she said,
- "It's time I went."

But she didn't move. Her eyes were more blue than green in the indoor light. The few minutes that followed remained, even in that day's immediate aftermath, hazy in my mind - glossed over for the audience's own good, like in films. All I can say is that I doubt the first move was mine. The next thing I recall clearly is Ermioni lying naked on my bed, her light brown hair loose, kissing me avidly on the mouth. I gazed on her as she lay relaxed afterwards. The village liked its women small and plump; Ermioni was tall and rangy - taller than myself, than most men in the village for that matter. As for her face, the jaw was a shade too angular, the mouth a little too wide, to be considered attractive. But the long, clean-cut lines from ankle to knee, knee to hip, hip to collar-bone, were lovely; and all of the sea was in her great figure-head's eyes. I said,

- "You're beautiful, Ermioni - d'you know?"

I wasn't thinking to please her; but I didn't expect the reproach in her eyes. I blushed with something like shame. Saying nothing, she got up, gathered her clothes from all around, got dressed. Before the wardrobe mirror she braided her hair, coiled it about her head, expertly knotted her kerchief. Her fingers were long, deft when they weren't nervous. She said, as if to her own reflection,

- "They want me to marry an old man and go to America."

I blurted, stupidly,

- "My father's in America."

She began to laugh. It was the first time I had seen her truly amused at something.

- "It's not your father, at any rate!"

Every time her laughter began to subside, another thought would cross her mind and set it off again. She was facing the mirror all the while. I laughed with her, once or twice, but my heart wasn't in it. Guilt

was beginning to build up inside me - the kind of guilt one feels at the sight of a person to whom one owes a lot of money which it will be impossible ever to repay. I said, miserably,
- "Are you going to?"
She turned to face me.
- "I'm going to give injections."
I was nonplussed, stared at her. She said, spelling it out, as though explaining a lesson to a particularly dim child,
- "When they're sick, people need injections. Sometimes for a long time, every day. The doctor only comes round once a month. He said he'll teach me."
An image of Ermioni and the doctor standing close beside each other flashed through my mind, followed, right on cue, by a pang of jealousy. Ermioni wasn't quite quick enough in veiling the gleam of triumph in her eyes. Suddenly I was in a rage. She saw it; and turning, walked quickly out of the house. Neither of us said goodbye.
After she left I lay back down on the bed, restless and dissatisfied. I meant to think things through, but instead I fell asleep and began dreaming. In the dream my father hadn't yet gone to America, and my mother was still alive. The three of us were picking olives; suddenly I saw that the canvas sheeting spread on the ground to catch the fruit as it was shaken off the tree was writhing with snakes. My mother saw it too, and so did my father; but while she and I were terrified, he seemed to treat it as a joke, gesticulating and laughing. I

told my mother that I was going to call Angelou, and started off running. But she said, "No, what we need is your grandmother's beehive!" I understood that she meant the beehive my grandmother had brought as a gift when I was still a child; and, changing course, I made for our house. When I got there I dashed to the back, but the beehive wasn't there. As I continued to search for it frantically, the sky grew dark; I felt the wind rise, carrying with it the first drops of rain. I was desperate; my mother would be dead and my father gone if I didn't get back to the olive-grove in time. The rain, coming down in torrents now, drenched my face. I woke up to find my cheeks wet with tears, and storm clouds beginning to obscure the sunshine outside.

I fetched some wood from outside and set some kindling in the small fire-place in the main room. My mother used to do all her cooking there. Her face, as it had come to me in my dream, haunted me: young, and afraid.

The year she died was the blackest of my life. I was sixteen; the Easter holidays were due in about two weeks' time, and I was at boarding-school in the capital counting the days, when the call came one day around noon for me to go to the headmaster's study. Since the previous summer, my mother hadn't been well; she had lost weight, and, though she didn't complain about it, it was obvious she was in pain. Just after the New Year, my father took her to a doctor in the nearest town; they came back from that journey, I remember, with drawn faces, and for the next few days both spoke very little.

As soon as I saw my father sitting there waiting, unshaven and broken-backed, I knew. He stood up and embraced me, while the headmaster, an Englishman of the stiff-upper-lip school, coughed and looked away. My father said nothing, and neither did I. We packed my suitcase together and took the bus back to the village - at that time a gruelling six-hour trip on dirt roads full of pot-holes. We buried my mother the next morning. Hadjimbey didn't come; but when he tried to prevent my grandmother from being at the funeral, the bloated mountain of flesh she had become finally rebelled, and she stood in the courtyard howling with such inhuman sounds that the village women who heard her took pity and braved her husband's possible wrath to go and fetch her. In the event, he didn't bar their way. At the cemetery Lefki stood by the open grave tearing her wispy white hair and keening, and when the coffin was lowered into the pit she tried to clamber down after the plain wooden box and had to be forcibly restrained. She outlived Constantia by three months to the day; the servants who found her dead in her bed one morning said, crossing themselves as they recounted it, they had never before seen such a happy smile on a cadaver's face.

At sixteen, I wasn't a child any more, but neither was I a man yet. My mother's death destroyed the world as I thought I knew it. I was going through a phase of reading voraciously, and was working my way through the school library more or less at random; by day my head was full of characters from Dickens, or

Greek mythology, or Shakespeare, or Jules Verne, and by night I lusted after Emile Zola's Nana, a cheap edition of whose adventures was doing the rounds of the boarding-house dormitory. All this had given me the notion that lives enjoyed plot and meaning; but my mother's death made no sense to me. If I could have viewed it as tragedy, that might have helped me accept it, but it struck me only as absurdity: to be born, live a mere thirty-three years, then die, was not to have had a life.

My own life was in effect just beginning; I took it desperately seriously, and wondered what I was going to do with it. My schoolmates were for the most part good, tractable boys, looking forward with meek equanimity to careers as doctors, lawyers, senior civil servants and the like. Up until that moment I hadn't thought about it much, but now, rebellious as I felt and angry, the thought of that kind of well-ordered future filled me with contempt bordering on panic. To inhabit a suit for a time, then - goodbye! It was monstrous.

Furthermore, a white-collar future seemed utterly alien to what had gone before in my life. Had I reasoned things out in a state of mind less hot-headed and furious, I would have realized that, of course, it was *meant* to be utterly alien - the idea behind the education afforded by a "fancy school", as Angelou was later to put it, was to move beyond village society and the lowly status of shepherd or farmer. That life was gone forever as an option; I had simply been educated out of it. I couldn't go back - and I didn't want to go forward.

Suicide presented itself briefly as a way out, but only as it does to those who don't really mean it. That is to say, I had romantic notions of being found on the beach in the early morning, picturesquely drowned, or of downing poison while reading verse, and the like. The catch was, I dreaded physical suffering; also, I still sneakingly clung to the notion that my life was a story, with beginning, middle and end, and I wanted to know how it would come out. Cutting it short now would be cheating myself, as it were, of the show.

So I turned more than ever to non-fatal forms of escape, like reading, and, every Saturday afternoon, going into town with friends to see a shadow theatre performance. Those were high times for the shadow theatre. There were three major companies in the capital, each quite distinct in style, each set of figurines and each play bearing the unmistakeable stamp of a particular shadow theatre master. My favourite was Odysseas Kamenos: his figurines were exquisitely simple, yet so well-articulated as to seem alive, and the plots they featured in were completely Kamenos' own, a frequently marvellous blend of the real and the magical - of what actually did happen in life, and what one scarcely dared hope might happen.

My mother had been dead two years when the headmaster summoned me once again to his study, this time to inform me that five government scholarships for university studies abroad were being made available, and that he felt confident on the basis of my academic performance that I could compete successfully for the one in Classics. I said, my heart in my mouth,

- "N-no, thank you, sir."

He looked astonished.

- "No, thank you?"

- "No, thank you."

- "But my boy! Whatever do you mean - no thank you?"

- "I - I don't wish to apply, sir. I mean, I don't want to go abroad to study."

His brow cleared.

- "Oh, I see! I see! Afraid of being homesick, eh? Not to worry, not to worry. The scholarships expressly stipulate repatriation after obtaining one's degree - and what's three years? Pff! Gone before you know it. Nothing."

He began to rummage in his desk drawer for the application forms, continuing to make soothing noises. I screwed up all my remaining courage.

- "Please sir - I really don't want to."

Once again, he stared at me, mouth a little open this time.

- "But Salih! Are you serious? What will you do if you don't continue with your studies?"

- "I want to be a shadow theatre master!"

Something quite beyond me had made my lips frame the reply; I was as amazed as he was, but there was nothing for it now. I was determined not to back down. The headmaster himself was apoplectic. Never before had a pupil, and an impoverished village bursary pupil at that, displayed such temerity.

- "Shadow theatre?! Shadow - ! But - but - you'll be no better than a gypsy!"

No doubt he meant to evoke rootlessness and indigence; but I immediately pictured moons, guitars and girls with pomegranate breasts. With an intimation of joy, I began to see the sense of my own reply.

- "Yes, sir. I mean, no sir, it's not like that, sir. It's an art, you see. If I - "

But he had had enough.

- "When I wish to hear a lecture on the shadow theatre as an art form, I shall let you know. You have proved a disappointment to me, to your school, and no doubt to your parents. Ahem. Your father. Dismissed!"

He stood with his back turned, gazing through the window at the acacias in bloom, as I left the study.

The following Saturday, after the show, I went to see Kamenos. I found him sitting in a room in the back, the walls hung with figurines, drinking brandy and eating salted almonds. He was burly, not too tall. One wouldn't have guessed that those large, meaty hands could manoeuvre the cardboard figurines so delicately. He raised his great head, covered with short curly hair like a bull's. It was pepper-and-salt grey; I guessed him to be about fifty.

- "Schoolboy! Evviva!"

He raised the brandy glass in a salute, gestured with it.

- "Sit you down!"

I sat, took off my school cap. He looked at me askance, a little curious, not very.

- "I've seen you! You come a lot. Right?

I nodded.

- "Name?"
- "Salih. Avraam."

He smiled a broad, delighted smile, gap-toothed like a child's.

- "A little of this - and a little of that - eh? I like it!"

He raised his glass.

- "That's what a person needs to get by! A little of this," he took a sip, "and a little of that!" He popped a salted almond, triumphantly, into his mouth. Then, turning to me,

- "You want to see how it's done. Right?"
- "I want to learn how to do it."

My voice was not entirely steady.

- "Ah!"

He leaned back in his chair. He was suddenly serious; but a small flame flickered in his black eyes. He tamped it down.

- "And your studies?"
- "No studies."
- "No studies! And why?"

I shrugged.

- "Just no."

The effect was that of an earthquake. He stood up, knocking the chair over, he shook his fists; he bellowed.

- "'Just no'! 'Just no'! What do you mean - WHAT DO YOU MEAN? Don't you tell me 'just no'! Don't you dare tell me! You say! Eh? You say!"

I was terrified - humiliated. I cast around for the right words, desperate to pacify him.

- "To study - I'd have to leave, go away. Thousands of miles. I wouldn't come back for years. My mother died - "

To my horror, scalding tears suddenly rushed to my eyes. I couldn't go on. But I had said enough, apparently, to appease him. He sat down. His voice, thunderous a moment ago, was conciliatory.

- "All right - all right. I don't want your life story."

He laid a paw on my shoulder.

- "You love the place you come from - you don't want to leave it. Right?"

I nodded.

He leaped up, extended the paw.

- "Shake on it! I'm with you."

I let my hand be crushed. He sat back down, refilled the brandy glass. He filled another, pushed it down the table towards me.

- "See - you've got to know why you're doing things. Studies - they're important. Not like deciding, are you going to eat broad beans or lentils tonight. No studies - fine. But you've got to know why!"

He sat for a while, nursing his drink, head bowed. He said, still gazing into the brandy,
- "Just one 'but'!"
He raised his eyes to meet mine.
- "This place you love - it might not repay you in kind."

I didn't know what to say. The conversation had left me exhausted. I longed for it to be over, but couldn't bring myself to leave with an arrangement between the two of us still unsettled. To my enormous relief, he suddenly turned practical.
- "Tell you what. How much school's left?"
- "Three months."
- "Three months. Right. You finish up, you go home, you talk to your father. Your father's still alive - hm?"

I nodded. I was exultant; I had never felt exhausted.
- "Right. You get his permission, then you come back. We'll do the villages together. The summer's when I travel around. As we go, you'll learn. When you've learned enough – you'll go!"

At that, he laughed uproariously. I said, starting to get up,
- "Fine!"
This sent him into fresh gales of laughter.
- "'Fine', he says - 'fine'! What 'fine', you idiot? What 'fine'? Ask me what I'm going to pay you - then say 'fine'! What am I going to pay you - eh?"

The nonchalance I was attempting evaporated. I felt my face grow scarlet.

- "Em...what will you pay me?"

He was back to bellowing.

- "Nothing, you idiot! I'm going to pay you NO-THING! What do you know, that *I* should pay *you*? *You'll* pay *me*, get it? To teach you the shadow theatre! With your attention! And I mean, A-TTEN-TION! And thirty pounds. You got thirty pounds?"

My heart had sunk through the floor.

- "Thirty pounds? N-no."

- "Too bad. You'll have to get it. Thirty pounds: that's for my teaching you the trade, plus bed, board and cigarettes. And travel. Finito!"

He poured yet another glass of brandy, chuckling. I hadn't touched mine. He raised the amber liquid, eyed me.

- "That's it then! Goodbye!"

I grabbed my cap and beat a hasty retreat. His roaring laugh followed me through the theatre and into the street; in my dreams, he laughed all night.

Chapter Nine

The women's coffee shop was full. It was early September; the reaping and threshing were over and the olive harvest hadn't yet started, so the patrons had some time on their hands. Angelou was busy making coffee, fetching and carrying cups and glasses; as she worked she dodged playing children and, occasionally, the cat Pulcheria, dislodged from one chair by a new arrival and on her way to another.

    The conversation had got around to the subject of giving birth, and the women were vying with each other as to who could come up with the most horrifying story. The midwife told about the time she had seen a fish, complete with gills and a tail, emerge from a mother's belly; someone else topped it with an account of how her great-grandmother had produced two devils joined together at the head, who screamed for several days then died. Her audience crossed themselves and shivered. Then young Xenia, Mayor Leonidas' daughter, who was pregnant with her first child, came in, and by tacit consent the subject was dropped.

    The talk, which had been general, broke up into groups and became desultory. It was late afternoon; one by one, the women prepared to leave, recalling ironing to be done, cows to be milked, supper to be prepared. The younger ones gathered their children about them, the older ones cautiously eased aching joints back into a standing position. By the time Ermioni strode in, looking tired and lankier than ever, the only women left besides Angelou were Xenia, who by virtue of being a cosseted only daughter in her eighth month of pregnancy was expressly barred from all household chores, and Liza, who was, so to speak, on holiday, her trawler captain husband and teenage sons being away on a fishing expedition.

Ermioni issued a monosyllabic greeting, set her leather satchel on a table, and sat down. A split second later she jumped up again; simultaneously a cacophonous flurry of grey fur shot off the chair as Pulcheria let it be known that she did not appreciate being sat on. The other three women began to laugh; Ermioni scowled, hissing disgustedly through her teeth.

- "Goddamn animal!"

Angelou, wiping tears of amusement from her eyes, went to the stove, began to prepare camomile tea. Ermioni, mollified by the sweet aroma wafting across the room, settled back down in her chair, rubbed her eyes with bony knuckles. She called, without looking at Angelou,

- "Put some honey in it, will you?"

Angelou set down a large china cup decorated with forget-me-nots before her friend, clicked a spoon around the steaming green liquid.

- "There you go."

Before picking up the drink, Ermioni wrapped her fingers around the cup, warming the stiffness out of the joints; lately, she had felt the beginnings of arthritis. Her mother had it, and her grandmother. In another fifteen, twenty years her hands would be as contorted and near-useless as theirs.

Angelou said, sympathetically,

- "Tired?"

- "Had to go rescue the old goat two nights in a row."

- "Still the diabetes?"

- "That's all he complains to me about, at any rate. Heart, too, though, by what the doctor says. And his lungs shot to hell. Why he hasn't kicked the bucket yet, I'll never know."

Angelou gave an imperceptible start. For Avraam's sake, she had often wished Hadjimbey dead; but somehow it was a shock to think that he might one day actually die. The only blood relative of Avraam's left....

Young Xenia interrupted them, curious.

- "Who's the old goat?"

Liza, who had guessed, said,

- "Hadjimbey. Right? I heard he was sick."

Ermioni's lips were set in a bitter line.

- "Sick he may be, but his mind's still on money!"

Xenia, big-eyed, said,

- "Why?"

Ermioni eyed Angelou as she answered.

- "Both yesterday and the day before, the man he's selling that land to had been there. They're arguing about the price - that's why the old guy got sick, from drinking all those cups of sweet coffee and smoking cigarettes for hours. Man was coming back today with his final offer. According to the servants."

For Ermioni, this was quite an oration. Angelou had never seen her so incensed.

Xenia said, with the air of a schoolgirl reciting a lesson,

- "They're going to build a hotel there, my father says. My father says that's capitalism, and it's bad, but at least there'll be some jobs for the people, so it's all right. That's what my father says, anyway."

She stopped, unsure whether she had praised or damned Hadjimbey's project.

Liza cut in, laughing,

- "There'll be more than jobs for the people - you wait! They built a hotel like that down Eleou way, where the long beach is, you know, and my cousin who married a girl from down there says in the summer it's full of naked foreign women. The men go crazy, he says, the wives hardly see their husbands' nether parts from May to October. Bathing naked he says - can you imagine?"

Liza, far from sounding indignant, was still laughing. She was plump and dimpled, and wasn't afraid of losing the captain to foreign women. Her sons, maybe; but cubs have to cut their teeth somewhere.

In Angelou's mind, an idea began to germinate. She let it. Xenia was agog.

- "Naked all over?"

- "With their tits hanging out all over the place anyway. They cover themselves with oil, my cousin says, and lie there roasting in the sun for hours, like chickens on a spit. They like to - "

- "Whose tits are hanging out?"

The question came from the door. The new client was Elenara, a middle-aged farmer's wife with a ready gold-toothed smile, whose five children, it was said, had been fathered by as many lovers. Elenara's husband Pepis, a small, friendly man with one leg a little shorter than the other, still called his wife "my partridge" after thirty years of marriage. His equanimity regarding the subject of Elenara's virtue was legendary. Once, a nosy woman neighbour had taken it upon herself to apprise the little farmer of his wife's misdemeanours. Pepis heard the busybody out politely and reflected for the merest instant before responding with inimitable finality:

- "Well, neighbour, if she did, she did, and if she didn't, she didn't!"

Liza brought Elenara in on the conversation.

- "The tits of the foreign women over in Eleou are hanging out! At that new hotel they built."

Young Xenia's curiosity was even more acute now.

- "But what about their husbands and their fathers? How come they let them do it?"

Liza was stumped for an instant; but Elenara picked up the slack.

- "They don't have to ask their fathers or their husbands to do anything. It's different, where they come from. I heard the men put on aprons and wash the dishes even!"

Angelou and Ermioni laughed; Xenia was, finally, reduced to speechlessness. Liza said, scornfully,

- "Imagine, your husband underfoot when you're trying to set your house in order! What man knows how to wash the dishes properly?"

Elenara gave her a knowing gold smile.

- "He wouldn't be underfoot. Your feet would be out of the house with the rest of you, doing other things."

Liza was still unconvinced.

- "What other things? What's a woman going to do out of the house anyhow, be a navvy?"

- "She could be a nurse."

Ermioni spoke softly, without emphasis; but her words suddenly arrested the conversation. For the space of a few minutes, the women sat silent, each turning over in her own mind the possibilities which had suddenly raised themselves.

Angelou picked up the thread of Ermioni's unspoken argument.

- "Or a shop-keeper."

Ermioni looked at her and smiled.

- "Or a shop-keeper."

Xenia had found her tongue again.

- "Or a film star!"

Elenara threw back her head, slapped her hand on her thigh.

- "Now you're talking!"

The conversation turned to the village cinema and its current offering, a lachrymose Indian love story whose plot reminded Angelou of certain of Mehmet Salih's more baroque efforts. As she made coffee for Elenara she reflected on how the coming of the cinema in the 'fifties had marked the beginning of the end of the shadow theatre. Neither she nor Avraam had wanted to admit it. He struggled on - there was still a market for shadow theatre performances at village fairs - but deep down they both knew it was a lost cause. The final blow, as if one were needed, was dealt by television, after independence. She sighed imperceptibly; she didn't feel like laughing any more. When Angelou rejoined the group Ermioni saw that the expression on the coffee shop keeper's lips was that of a person in pain.

Outside, the sun had gone down, giving way to the brief Mediterranean dusk. It would soon be night. Seeing Liza get up to leave, young Xenia hoisted her belly with effort off the chair.

- "Can I go with you? I'm scared of the dark alone."

The two women went out. Elenara stayed on for half an hour, joking and reading her own fortune in the coffee-grounds, before leaving in turn. Alone, Angelou and Ermioni sat silent on opposite sides of the same table. The room, imperfectly lit by a pressure-lamp, was full of shadows.

- "Are you going to tell me?"

Angelou, lost in thought, gave a start at the sound of Ermioni's voice.

- "Tell you what?"
- "What happened to him."

There was another silence. Finally Angelou said, slowly,

- "He was knifed."

Ermioni flinched slightly at the word, then became immobile as a statue. Her eyes, now the grey-green colour of sea-weed still wet from the receding tide, stared down at her own hands lying inert, one on top of the other, on the wooden table. Angelou studied her closely for a few moments; then, with a sudden expulsion of breath, she leaned back in her chair and said,

- "You slept with him, didn't you."

It was a statement, not a question. Ermioni hesitated a fraction of a second; then she shrugged. She still didn't look at Angelou.

The coffee shop keeper stood up abruptly, lips tight. With jerky movements she walked to the cabinet, took out a glass and a bottle of brandy. Her back to Ermioni she downed a shot, poured another. She said, as if to herself,

- "I should have known."

Then, her voice louder and harsher,

- "How long?"

- "From the beginning. Every once in a while."
Ermioni's tone had turned sullen.
- "And us?"
The lay nurse shrugged again.
- "Us was us."

Angelou downed the second shot of brandy, poured a third. She said, staring hard at Ermioni, her black eyes burning,
- "To hell and beyond with your faithless cunt!"
Ermioni rounded on her.
- "What do you care anyway! It wasn't as if he loved me! It was you all along! I shoved myself between his sheets and he helped himself - what man wouldn't? And so what?"
Angelou ignored all her statements but one.
- "And what about us then? Did you help yourself just because I shoved myself at you?"
- "You said it, not me."

By way of a response, Angelou flung the glass she held across the room, where it shattered against a wall. Ermioni, though the missile was not directed at her, ducked involuntarily. She watched warily as Angelou, face set, marched back to the cabinet and picked up another glass. The coffee shop keeper fixed the nurse with a hard black stare.
- "Did he know?"

Ermioni, relieved that Angelou seemed for the moment to have stopped throwing things, gave a bitter laugh.

- "Him? About you and me? He was asleep on his feet. Always thinking up stories for his precious theatre, right? The end of the world might have come and he wouldn't have noticed."
- "Bollocks!"

Angelou's face was flushed dark crimson under its deep tan.

- "Like hell it's bollocks!"
- "Bollocks! Avraam knew more about what was going on than you ever will!"
- "He was asleep on his feet!"
- "If you thought he was such an idiot, what did you chase after him for then?"

Ermioni shot Angelou a look of pure hatred.

- "Nice of you to put it that way!"

Angelou raised her glass in a mock toast.

- "Nice of you to think him an idiot!"

The brandy glass in her hand, she began to march around the room; as though afraid of what it might do, she thrust her one free hand savagely into a pocket. When she had gone around several times she said,

- "Are you going back to Hadjimbey's?"

Her voice, though a shade unnatural, was suddenly free of ire. Ermioni looked at her, startled by the abrupt shift in the conversation. She thought fast, decided to accept the implied cease-fire.

- "In the morning, first thing."
- "Can you find out if he sold the land?"
- "Yes."
- "Tell me as soon as you can."

- "What - ?"

Angelou shot her a look, and the question died on her lips.

- "Just find out."

She walked over to the brandy bottle, poured herself another drink. Ermioni hesitated, then said,

- "You'll wreck your liver."

A second black-eyed look from Angelou once again reduced the lay nurse to silence. Ermioni got up, retrieved the satchel.

- "Good night."

Angelou didn't reply. As the rangy figure vanished into the darkness outside, the coffee shop keeper picked up the brandy bottle, looked at it, and moved slowly towards one of the tables. Pulcheria, appearing from the shadows, gave one of her raucous greetings and rubbed herself against Angelou's legs. Then the cat, too, stepped outside and melted into the night.

For the second time since Avraam Salih's death, Angelou woke up in the middle of the morning from a brandy sleep with a dry tongue and throbbing temples. Once again her first move, when movement became possible, was in the direction of the cooking-stove; once more, her first task fumblingly to brew a cup of strong, steaming coffee. She was about to pour it when there was a timid knock at the door; in response to her hoarse "Come in!" a young girl of about fourteen with a mass of dark curly hair and a tear-stained face came inside. Angelou knew her; it was Nina, the eldest of the widow

Laoura's seven children. The family was one of the poorest in the village; Angelou recalled Ermioni saying that the eldest girl had gone to work as a servant in Hadjimbey's house.

- "What's the matter?"

The coffee shop keeper, bleary-eyed as she was, kept her gaze fastened on Nina's distraught face. The girl's hair was tousled; through her thin cotton dress her small breasts heaved with suppressed sobs.

Wordlessly, Nina sat down and, folding her arms on the table before her, lowered her face onto them and began to cry. Angelou let her be for a few moments while she brewed a second cup of coffee; then, walking back to the table, she sat down and extended the hot drink towards the bowed head. After a few more shuddering sobs Nina looked up, blew her nose on a handkerchief proffered by Angelou, made an effort to stop crying. Her lips still quivered as she said,

- "He put his hands on me."

Angelou understood. The old satyr liked them younger and younger these days, it seemed. She said,

- "Hadjimbey?"

But she knew very well, even before Nina's miserable little nod of the head, that it was, indeed, Hadjimbey.

Reflectively, she drank some coffee; made Nina do the same. When the girl was a little calmer, Angelou said,

- "Why'd you come here? Why didn't you go to your mother?"

- "I can't tell my mother!" The dark eyes, almost as dark as Angelou's own, filled with tears again; but, with a supreme effort, Nina fought them back. Her voice was very husky as she continued. "Anyway, I heard some things - I thought you would - I thought I should - "

Angelou sat stock still. She said, and as she said it, she had the oddest feeling that all this had happened before,

- "What things?"

Nina was excited now; one might almost think she had forgotten the unwelcome hands and where they had been placed.

- "About Avraam Salih. I heard Hadjimbey talking to the foreman, I mean they didn't know I was there. Something about taking Avraam Salih's body somewhere. And then the foreman went off in the car. That's all. He was your friend – so I thought - "

The girl's voice faltered before Angelou's immobility, and her face threatened once more to crumple; but before a fresh torrent of grief could drown Nina's tale, Angelou had roused herself and put a comforting hand on the slight young shoulder.

- "It's all right. You did the right thing. Now listen - never, ever repeat what you just told me to anyone. Not your mother, not anyone. Promise?"

Nina nodded, her dark eyes now wide. Angelou got up, went into the adjacent store-room, began filling several brown paper bags from the contents of sacks and barrels. In a few minutes she emerged and walked up to Nina.

- "Here's some sugar and flour. And beans. Oh, and here's some coffee too."

She deposited the bags on the table before the astonished girl, sat down again.

- "Look. Don't go back to Hadjimbey's. How much does he pay you?"

Nina, nonplussed, stammered a sum. It was pitiful. Angelou said,

- "I'll pay you twice that, plus groceries. To mind the coffee shop when I'm on my rounds, and clean the place every morning. All right? Tell your mother I asked you - tell her that's why you're leaving Hadjimbey's. Nothing else, d'you understand? It's very dangerous. D'you understand?"

Angelou's voice was urgent, almost fearful; but Nina was beaming now, teeth white in her brown half-child, half-woman's face. She scrambled up from her chair, cradling the bags against her bosom as one would a baby.

- "I won't! Thanks Miss Angelou! Thanks!" And she was gone, almost dancing out of the door on delighted feet.

Angelou, getting up to call out "Tomorrow!" in the girl's wake, stepped outside just in time to see a red sports car pull up in the street in front of the Women's Coffee Shop sign. The driver, a modishly-dressed young man with a professional air and a worried expression, got out of the car and approached her.

- "Miss Angelou! Remember me? I came as soon as I could, I mean, when I heard - "

- "Come in Mr. Theo. Of course I remember you."

The young man from the television who was going to make Avraam Salih a film-star sat down, nervously lit a cigarette.

- "He's dead, right? I mean, it's true?" He glanced, questioningly at Angelou, continued without waiting for her reply. "I mean, the programme's in two months - the budget's been approved now, we can't cancel!"

His expensive imported cigarette only half-finished, he began to cast around for an ash-tray; Angelou, an unfathomable expression in her eyes, handed him one.

- "Coffee?"

- "Oh, don't bother - well, if you insist!"

But Mr. Theo's mind was not on coffee. With an absent "Your health," he took a sip, stubbed the cigarette out, lit another.

Angelou, who had sat down and was looking at him with an even gaze, said,

- "Maybe you could make your programme about something else."

- "Something else?" He still wasn't paying much attention, still smoking nervously.

- "Yes. How about a women's coffee shop? Wouldn't people like to hear about that?"

He stared at her; then something akin to realization began to play over the features of his face. He looked around the room, said with sudden interest,

- "You mean, this? This is a coffee shop for women?"

- "Right."

- "They come here? To drink coffee? Like the men?"

A gleam had appeared in Mr. Theo's eye. Angelou said,

- "Better than the men. They're going to stop something. A hotel."

- "You mean - ?"

He was at a loss again.

- "I mean someone's going to build a tourist hotel. The women don't want it. We're going to stop it."

Mr. Theo, who was not, appearances to the contrary, altogether slow-witted, had now got the idea. He stood up; the frown had vanished from his face.

- "Amazons! Lysistrata! We'll do it! I'll be back in a few days with the crew!"

He was already on his way out. Angelou got up; from the doorway she watched him get into the red sports car, drive off in a cloud of dust. He hadn't thanked Angelou for the coffee; he did not bother to wave goodbye.

She smiled a sour little smile and closed the door after the man from the television. Avraam Salih would have been amused, she thought to herself; television might have killed the shadow theatre, but it would be by television that the shadow theatre would finally achieve its aim.

Chapter Ten

Ermioni was wrong: I knew that Angelou and she were lovers. It happened like this. One day, I was on my way to the women's coffee shop to consult Angelou on our itinerary for the following week. It was mid-afternoon, siesta time, and I thought it more likely that I'd find her alone. Now here's a funny thing: I remember all this happening in deepest winter - I could swear to a north wind like a knife, and to feeling frozen to the bone. But in fact the door of the coffee shop was open, which was only the case in summer; and, come to think of it, I was dressed in light trousers and a short-sleeved shirt.

The open door was the reason I heard their voices before I actually saw them - Angelou and Ermioni, I mean, sitting across the table from each other, talking softly. Just like the very first time I had gone to the coffee shop, only now they weren't laughing, and they didn't see me. I stood there frozen, transfixed by Angelou's attitude. She was perfectly still; but with her whole self, she was tending towards Ermioni, a sort of visible motion of the soul which found its most eloquent expression in her radiant face, in her eyes, black, incandescent, devouring the other woman, utterly absorbed in her, utterly lost to the world - lost to me.

I stared and stared at her. I wanted to cry out - to howl with jealousy and rage; I thought I had actually done it, but, as in nightmares, my voice wouldn't come, and my face, just like my heart, had turned to stone. I hated Ermioni with every muscle and nerve and bone - with every atom of my being. If I were the killing sort, I would have killed her then and there. Instead I turned and ran like a man pursued by the furies, back through the village, past my own house to the little stone bridge just down the road. My legs were collapsing; I just managed to gain the parapet before they gave way altogether. Heart bursting, lungs on fire, I put my head in my hands, and sobbed like a lost child. The sun was almost down when I finally started to walk back home. I had one thought left - that neither Angelou nor Ermioni should ever know what I had seen or been through that day.

 Later that same summer Angelou spoke to me about her father, and about what had happened when she went to live with him again. It was late at night; we were at my house. She asked me not to light the pressure lamp, as though she wanted to annihilate in darkness the world she was speaking about - or was it her own self she wanted to erase? She spoke in a voice of pure pain - calm, and the more terrible for it. She never once said the word "father", only "he". She made it sound as though the word "father" was impossible to say. When she had finished, she gave a small sigh, and said,

 - "It goes on all the time."

That was all. I brought out a bottle of brandy and we sat drinking it in the dark; then we drank another. It reminded me of the time my father and I had sat drinking wine, saying goodbye without saying it. Something was lost, something else gained. That night, Angelou slept in my arms for the first and only time; and towards dawn it was her turn to cry. I rocked her out of her nightmare the way I remembered my mother doing when I was small, and wished I could make her a child again and restore to her a child's proper nightmares, about wolves and being lost in the forest, instead of the others, the unspeakable ones which had been forced on her. She had tried to speak to me about them, as she had not done, I was sure, to anyone else; and the resentment which had squatted in my gut like a malevolent toad since the day I had seen her and Ermioni together was banished, and I loved Angelou more than ever.

As I lay awake holding her, I thought about my own father. How was he, really, and what had he found at the end of that voyage of thousands of miles? I remembered him telling me he had decided to go to America, the day I arrived home at the end of my final school year. He was there waiting for me when I got off the bus; he insisted on carrying my suitcase, setting it down each time we met anyone the better to announce proudly,

- "Avraam's finished school! Top of the class!"

When we got home he said,

- "You wash up! I've got to fire up the oven!"

Lamb and potatoes baked as sweet and tender as Turkish delight in the outdoor clay oven was his specialty; this was the first time I had seen him make the dish - the first time I had seen him happy - since my mother died. In his joy, he looked a boy again. As he busied himself fetching wood, I studied the lean, humorous face, the rogueish black eyes, and thought I knew why Constantia had fallen in love with him. I didn't have the heart to tell him about the shadow theatre; I was sure my decision to turn down the Classics scholarship would be the disappointment of his life, and I didn't want to worry him with the problem of the thirty pounds. Thirty pounds! I had been racking my brains on how to lay my hands on what for those days was a minor fortune, and had come up dry.

Had I been less young and self-absorbed, I might have realized that my father was hatching announcements of his own. As it was, when he raised his glass over the remains of our feast, drank deeply, and fixed me with a look suddenly become grave, all I could think was that he had somehow guessed my guilty secret. His actual words almost knocked me off my chair.

- "I've decided to go to America."

I stared at him. What was he talking about? He was my father! Fathers didn't just up and go to America! I said, in a half-strangled voice,

- "America! But that's for young men!"

In response, he threw his head back and laughed.

- "Or widowers! Anyhow," he raised his glass with a slightly mocking expression, "I'm not that old, you know."

I fell silent, my head bowed. An overwhelming loneliness had come over me, as though my father were already gone. He leaned forward, a little anxious now.

- "Avraam! You'll be going off to study. Right? What will I do? I'm here all alone – without your mother – your grandparents are gone - it's not as though anyone needs me!"

His voice was pleading. I summoned up all my courage.

- "I'm not going to study."

I was afraid he would be angry; but for the moment he just looked at me. After a few minutes' silence, he said, enunciating each word slowly,

- "Come to America with me, then."

I shook my head. He continued to look at me thoughtfully.

- "Why not?"

- "Shadow theatre. Odysseas Kamenos said I could be his apprentice."

This time the silence lasted much longer. I sat watching my father's arm, lying immobile on the table. Finally, the arm began to shift; I was afraid that, for the first time ever, he was going to hit me, and flinched in advance. But his hand moved, not up and out towards my face, but to his wine glass. Lifting it, he said,

- "Here's to the shadow theatre! I never knew it was important; but I know it now."

In that moment, my father taught me that which had been the essence of his own life: tolerance, and respect for the other. I raised my own glass; we drank together, but I was drinking, not to the shadow theatre, but to my father, Mehmet Salih, a great man with a great heart in a world of so many small people. Now I understood even better why my mother had loved him - why all women had loved him; and that's when it came to me for the first time: that Zenon Hadjimbey, too, had loved him, before they had fallen out so irrevocably - that the love borne by the older man for the younger one was the reason why the rift between them had been so violent and so final. To be betrayed by one's henchman, that was one thing; to be betrayed by one's beloved son, quite another.

I raised my glass again and said,
- "Here's to America!"

He flashed his brilliant smile at me, and we drank again; then we began on another bottle. We both knew we were saying goodbye for ever.

It turned out that my father had been planning his departure for some time. His papers were ready; the ship sailed in a week. On the eve of his journey, as we were finishing a skimpy meal, he looked at me and said,
- "You'll need money."

He was telling me, not asking. I grew scarlet; I had vowed to myself that he should never know about my money problems. Had I been talking in my sleep? He smiled, then got up without a word and went to the walnut wardrobe. When he came back to the table, he was carrying something I had never seen before: a three-stranded necklace of gold coins, strung on a finely-wrought chain finished with an ornate clasp.

- "Your mother brought this with her when she left her father's house. It was the one thing - "

His eyes filled with tears. I put my hand over his, covering the necklace.

- "You'll need it, over there! How will you start out?"

He smiled.

- "I'm not starting out. You are. I'm continuing."

- "But - "

He turned my hand over, pressed the necklace into the palm.

- "It's for you. Your mother said so."

The next morning I got up with him before dawn, and we boarded the ramshackle village bus to the port. The sea was choppy, I remember, and the cries of the gulls circling overhead seemed to echo my own piercing, wordless grief. I told myself I was a grown man, set, after all, as my father had said, to embark on my own life; and that the time for clinging to my parents like a child was over. But the more I chastised myself the more orphaned and miserable I felt, until it seemed only a matter of moments before I burst into the tears of a six-year-old on his first day at school. Help arrived in the shape of an officious employee of the shipping company, who began to herd the passengers towards the landing-stage. The port was not a natural harbour, and the ship lay anchored a couple of miles offshore; a barge stood waiting to transport people and freight out to it.

I stood watching in the early morning sun as the wide-bellied open hull receded and the white patch like a postage-stamp that was my father's shirt grew less and less distinct, until it finally shrank into the merest pinpoint, and vanished. I was too heartsick to stay and watch the ship sail. I drank a cup of coffee at a place near the docks, then boarded the bus again and settled down to wait for its departure at noon. I fell asleep; and when I woke up the bus-driver was calling my name to let me know that the village lay just a short distance ahead, and that in a few moments we would be reaching my house. As I stepped inside the silence hit me like a blast of cold air. I searched out my own suitcase and began to pack. At that moment I didn't know whether I would ever be able to stand coming back to Ayia again.

When I got to the capital I went to find Kamenos after the show, as I had done the first time. He looked neither glad nor sorry to see me. I said,

- "Mr. Odysseas" – that's how he liked to be addressed - "Mr. Odysseas, I don't have thirty pounds, but I have this."

And I took the coin necklace out of my pocket. He glanced at it for the merest instant.

- "Bravo. Now put it away."

I was baffled.

- "But - I'll have to sell - "

- "PUT IT AWAY! Idiot! D'you think I really wanted your money - eh? "

I stared at him. He began to laugh.

- "Look at that face! Priceless! You really thought I'd skin you, didn't you? Who d'you take me for? Here I was, getting ready to come to your goat-village to find you if you didn't show up! It was a test, idiot! You passed! You'd sell your dead mother's necklace to become a shadow theatre master! You will become one! I salute you!"

He raised the inevitable glass of brandy in my direction, drank it in one gulp, then performed a sweeping bow to the floor. I managed a shaky smile.

When he was upright again, his face was serious.

- "Now look. Here's the kind of shadow theatre I do. Sit down! Now, here's how it is. I don't do patriotic stuff."

I started to say something, but he raised his hand for silence.

- "I don't do patriotic stuff. Why? I'll tell you."

He refilled his glass, grimaced with disgust at my untouched drink.

- "I was doing a play in a mixed village once, see? Christians and Moslems, sitting there. Suddenly one of the Moslems stands up and shouts, 'Mr. Odysseas, what are these plays for?' I was surprised, I'll tell you. I came out from behind the screen and I said, 'What the hell do you mean interrupting the performance with stupid questions? The plays are to amuse the audience. What else?' And d'you know what he said to me? He said,

'Well, we Moslems are audience too, and here are your boys in the play killing us like flies. We're supposed to be amused by that? Dropping dead all over the place without even a fight?' It stopped me in my tracks, hearing that, I'll tell you. So I said to him, 'Mr. Hassan, you're right; and I beg your pardon. Now, ladies and gentlemen, you will watch 'The Blackamoor' instead, where there's only one person who gets killed, and anyway it's suicide. And that's what they watched, 'The Blackamoor', and everybody was happy. So I don't do patriotic plays. You know 'The Blackamoor'?"

I said,

- "Not really."

- "It's a good play. There's a black man, he's a general and he's really brave, so when he falls in love with a noble white lady she falls right back, and they get married, and it's all lovey-dovey for a while; then some spiteful guy comes along and whispers in the Blackamoor's ear that supposedly the lady is cuckolding him, and he goes crazy with jealousy. Then, not to kill her, he kills himself! I tell you, they all go crazy for the scene where the lady comes in and there he is, stone dead with a knife stuck in his chest, for love. You really never heard of it? What's the matter?"

I was so excited, I had jumped out of my chair.

- "It's 'Othello'! Except - "

- "What 'Othello' and nonsense! It's the 'Blackamoor'!"

- "No, 'Othello'! By Shakespeare! Except Othello kills the lady, *then* he kills himself!"

Kamenos was by now enraged.

- "Well I don't read so good and I don't write any better and I don't know who this Shakespeare was, but I do know that if that's how he wrote it, he was wrong!"

The task of defending Shakespeare lent me courage.

- "He was not wrong! He wrote plays centuries ago and he was a genius!"

But Kamenos was not to be shaken.

- "He - was - wrong. The way you and this Shakespeare guy tell it, see, jealousy kills the lady and the Blackamoor. But the way I tell it, the Blackamoor kills jealousy; get it? He sees it coming - he sizes it up - and boom! He kills it the only way he can - by killing himself."

I sat back down in my chair and pondered this for a time. Despite myself, I was impressed by Kamenos' analysis. I said, half to myself,

- "*The green-eyed monster.*"
- "What?"

He was suspicious again.

- "*The green-eyed monster.* That's what Shakespeare called jealousy."

Kamenos suddenly smiled his broad, gap-toothed smile.

- "Good! Good! Did he write anything else?"

I struggled not to laugh.

- "A lot."
- "We'll do them, then!"

He was as good as his word; over the next few months, "Macbeth" ("The Ghost"), "Romeo and Juliet" ("The Lovers") and "A Midsummer Night's Dream" ("The Ass") became part of our repertory. Admittedly, Kamenos gave Shakespeare's plots short shrift: Lady Macbeth lost all her influence ("Who'd want to watch a play about some guy doing what his wife says?"), Romeo and Juliet survived to have children and grandchildren ("Too sad, killing them off like that), and Titania remained for ever in love with Bottom ("Funnier!"). But the spirit was the thing.

My apprenticeship with Odysseas Kamenos, shadow theatre master extraordinary, lasted two years, a super-gestation, a second birth into the life I was destined to lead until my death. There was no real hardship involved in learning the trade, except that of knowing myself to be an ignoramus, as clumsy with the puppets at first as a baby learning to spoon its pap. I had to swallow my pride then, grown quite advanced during all those years of being the cleverest boy in the class, and try and take Kamenos' mocking insults with equanimity, or at least something resembling it sufficiently to fool him. Not that it did, he was too sharp for that, but he let it pass. What he couldn't abide was inattention; if he ever sensed that I was giving a particular thing he was trying to teach me anything less than my whole self, he would explode. For the next several days I might as well have been a pet dog caught stealing the Sunday roast, such was the disgrace I would have fallen into. Then I would please him with some small first-time accomplishment, and he would start to talk to me again.

We travelled constantly, staging performances in I don't know how many villages during that first summer. My body was sore from the hours spent rattling over the pothole-ridden roads in hot, dusty buses, and I grew to be an expert on inns, recognizing at a glance which were likely to offer the company of bedbugs with the room, and which not. As long as the food was good, I didn't mind the vermin so much; Kamenos, being an epic eater, made sure it was good, too, and plentiful. He could devour spare ribs by the dozen at one sitting, would scoff if the landlord had the temerity to set merely a single chicken before him or if the quantities of potatoes and bread accompanying the meat were anything less than gargantuan. I would have finished my own meal long since, and he would still be sitting there, calling for more wine, heaping more food on his plate, unabashed and unabating.

Noticing the look on my face he would roar,

- "What's the matter? You sick, or something? Call that eating?"

And he would laugh uproariously, and order another loaf of bread. He literally ate and drank all his earnings; clothes he cared not one jot about, he had neither wife nor children that I knew of, and certainly he didn't save a penny.

There were some who thought Odysseas Kamenos a traitor, because of his refusal to do the 'patriotic stuff'. No glorious 1821, no latter-day heroes setting fire to the Governor's Mansion in the bid to oust the country's colonial masters. Occasionally, a member of the audience would heckle and demand a play of the sort; then Kamenos would stop the performance, and explain politely that he did not favour works about hatred and killing. Once, a protester asked heatedly,

- "But Mr. Odysseas! Don't you want to the people to be free?"

To which he replied,

- "I want them to be free from hatred and killing!"

To me, later, he said,

- "Don't think it's easy. I like a hero as well as the next man, and those boys who fought the Turks in '21 and who go out and toss the bombs at the Colonials now, well, they got tired of being slaves and I don't fault them for that. But look at what's happening here - Christians and Moslems pell-mell in one country, no sorting one out from the other, it's such a mix-up. If we start killing each other, we're sunk! Already the Colonials have got the idea, firing the Moslems up, telling them independence is for Christians and if they get it woe betide the Moslem community. I tell you, going about showing plays that set one against the other is playing with dynamite."

He sighed, then looked at me.

- "And what about you, then? Christian mother, Moslem father - what do you think? Eh?"

I grew pale. I was young, and didn't like to be reminded I was an oddity. Finally, my reluctant brain yielded an answer.

- "Maybe...maybe there could be plays about Christians and Moslems getting along. Like my mother and father - or something..."

My voice trailed off uncertainly, but Kamenos was grinning with all his gap-toothed might.

- "You got it! You got it! That's it, see? The shadow theatre can teach the people! It doesn't have to be about killing - it doesn't have to be about anything it damn well doesn't want to be about. Go to it, my boy! Go to it!"

Those words of his never left me; I went to it, once Kamenos had taught me the basics, as best I could. The first play I staged on my own was a love story between a Christian girl and a Moslem boy - my own parents' love story, with elements of Romeo and Juliet thrown in, for I had also learned from Kamenos that borrowing and adapting renders homage to the source quite as much as slavish adherence. Wherever I performed "Christina and Afif", before Christians or Moslems or both, there wasn't a dry eye in the house. Did it "teach the people"? I can't say. "He entertained, and did no harm": it seemed to me a good enough epitaph then, and it still does today.

"Entertained" - that was key; I don't want you to get the idea from all this that dry didacticism was what Kamenos went in for, and neither did I. The shadow theatre had to take people out of themselves, transpose them into an alternative world of the imagination which, for as long as the black shapes danced across the screen, felt more real somehow than the real; or it was nothing. In the end, cinema and television won out because they did it even better; no one understood that more keenly than I. But in those early, heady days as Kamenos' apprentice, I was the last one to see it coming.

After that, Kamenos and I saw each other unfailingly once a year - in August, when the journey to the monastery of the Virgin for the festival of the Assumption would take him through Ayia. The buses from the capital to the cape, where the monastery stood, used to break the long journey overnight in our village in those days, and Kamenos would spend the time at my house, drinking and talking till morning. Later he acquired a shabby car, of which he was inordinately proud and which gave him the option of stopping for as long or as little as he liked - sometimes a few days, sometimes just a couple of hours, as the mood took him.

It became our habit, when he had the time to spare, to mount a joint shadow theatre performance at the women's coffee shop; the men, out of pride, stayed away, which left Kamenos and myself free to stage far raunchier productions than would have been possible in the disapproving presence of husbands and fathers. The women were at first astonished, then delighted; and more discerning, it seemed to me, than their menfolk, when it came to the quality of the play. With the men, a certain amount of bravado and brouhaha could sometimes substitute for well-honed dialogue and action, but with the women the plot and quips had to be first rate, and the same went for the singing; otherwise they'd laugh and hiss the figurines off the stage and that would be the end of it.

Angelou, of course, never charged a fee for the use of the coffee shop; and, at my own insistence, the takings were always for Kamenos. The two of them - Kamenos and Angelou - hit it off from their very first meeting; and he would always insist on a song or two from the coffee shop keeper to round off the evening. When everyone else had gone home they would sit over a bottle, telling bawdy jokes and getting drunk together. I never could match Angelou drink for drink, but Kamenos could, and more; and when they were both finally so far gone that the jokes became incoherent and they were on the verge of an argument over whether Karagöz was stupid, or in fact very intelligent, I would step in and haul Kamenos off to my house to sleep it all off. It was he who first dubbed Angelou 'Black-Eyes' - a compliment to her eyes and a play on the word 'Karagöz' all in one.

- "Next year, Black-Eyes! I salute you!"

And he would sing, "Come girl and show us your eyes so black" at the top of his voice all the drunken way to bed.

He liked sleeping on the roof - the coolest place during the hot, humid summer nights. We would lie flat on our backs on straw mats and try to count the stars, laughing at everything and nothing, until we fell asleep. Odysseas Kamenos was my second father; to him I owed this hand-to-mouth, marginal, enchanted life, which seduced me to the end, and made me happy.

Chapter Eleven

It was early morning, beginning of November: the sky was overcast, with the threat of rain. The door of the women's coffee shop was shut against the chill. Inside, under the watchful gaze of Pulcheria, Angelou was gathering together the makings of lunch in the open: loaves of bread, sheep's milk cheese, olives, tins of corned beef. The women's protest had been under way one full week, and its success was, literally, spectacular - dominating the nation's television screens during the evening news, transfixing everyone from government ministers to the smallest child. Even the President himself, it was said, sat each night in front of his set, mesmerized by the images of the women standing calm and implacable before the hungry rumble of the machines and the barely-controlled hysteria of the site manager, the more pressured by virtue of being flanked by the developer, the developer's men, and a phalanx of impotent construction workers wearing sheepish smiles, as much as to say:

- "Think of it, all this muscle defeated by a bunch of soft tits!"

On the third day, another player joined the drama: Hadjimbey himself, smoked out of his lair into quite extraordinary visibility, blank sunglasses defying the camera even as his enormous, baldly glinting head inevitably courted it, thin lips set and jowls shaking with a rage which he did not bother to disguise. But, more than any other figure, it was Angelou who seized the viewers' imagination - a woman become a rock, or a century-old tree, so immutably fixed did she seem on the first morning at the head of the protesters, black eyes fiery in a face grown ageless, sexless, with the distilled passion she brought to the enterprise; her enterprise, from start to finish, even if inside herself secretly she thought of it as Avraam Salih's work. An enterprise on which she had staked, it was plain to see as she stood inches away from the menacing treads of the bulldozer, her very life. The lone human being against the machine: the confrontation was mythic, and not to be denied.

    At the start, the mass she led numbered six or seven hundred, and included every able-bodied female in the village. Old crones, buxom brides who had hung up their wedding wreaths over the marriage bed just days before, harassed mothers of ten, little gap-toothed girls in pigtails - Angelou had succeeded in drafting them all. If their movement was not marked by unity of purpose - some really feared losing their men to an influx of promiscuous foreign blondes, others simply revelled in the novel role of female rebel - it enjoyed, at any rate, determination and unity of action. As the site manager, in a first unsuccessful bid to overcome the opposition, ordered the drivers to rev up the excavators and bulldozers and make as if to charge at the demonstrators, not one woman fainted or panicked or turned on Angelou for having put all of them in danger. These acts of courage were then repeated that same night in a domestic setting, as husbands and brothers and fathers threatened and thundered and, in some instances, raised their hand to their women, in an effort to prevent wives and daughters and sisters from going back out to the hotel site the next day.

If the truth be told, the men's assertions of authority were half-hearted; who could object to a scheme which had made heroes of everyone in the village overnight, and that before the entire nation? The ubiquitous Mr. Theo, dashing about, camera crew in tow, interviewing anyone within range of his microphone, had done his job well, managing to convey the fact that the protest was the work of women without, for all that, creating the impression that the males of the village were redundant drones.

- "Mr. Mayor! The women could not have done this without your moral support! Could we have a few words?"

- "Sir! Your wife and sister would not have felt safe enough to participate in this protest without knowing you are there to protect them in case of trouble. The nation would like to hear your views!"

After the first day, the women did their part to help mollify their menfolk by setting up a rota system which kept the protest going while also ensuring that the housework got done and the children, the men themselves and the elderly were fed and cared for; so that, at any given moment of the day, Angelou could count on a critical mass of two or three hundred women being there to back her up.

The police were, of course, called, and the police came, but to no great effect. The sergeant ordered his men to ring the protesters, then stood helpless as to what to do next, for the order had come from higher up: the government did not want to be seen mistreating women and crushing by force a protest which, if the barrage of nightly telephone calls from ordinary citizens to the television headquarters was any indication, enjoyed overwhelming sympathy among the public.

At one point, the journalist Osman also appeared in the beetle-black Morris known to Angelou, a photographer accompanying him as before. He did not address her, but asked whether any of the workers were Moslem, spoke briefly to the three who came forward, and, after instructing the photographer to take this or that shot, left by the way he had come. The fruit of his labours proved to be a front-page piece in the next day's edition of "Hakikat", carrying the headline: "Moslem Workers: How Are We To Feed Our Families?" The story sternly called on the government to halt the protest, which threatened the livelihood of Moslem construction workers, besides constituting a breakdown of law and order. An editorial on the inside pages posed the question: "If the government is not capable of controlling a gaggle of rowdy females in aprons, how can it possibly control the well-armed extremist elements whose goal is the extermination of the country's Moslem community?"

After a few hours, at any rate, the police force more or less disbanded and joined the construction workers in chain-smoking and ogling the prettier of the protesters, who were not, it must be said, entirely unresponsive. Only Angelou shunned the male assemblage entirely, speaking to the sergeant or the site manager only when absolutely necessary, and turning her back pointedly on Zenon Hadjimbey whenever he appeared on the scene.

Now, as she began to pack the provisions in baskets, the sound of footsteps outside the coffee shop door caused her to stop and listen; an instant later Zenon Hadjimbey stood framed in the doorway, clad in his usual paramilitary costume: khaki trousers, black shirt, black leather belt and high boots. He did not remove his sunglasses on coming in out of the light. Behind him, Angelou made out the developer, a florid man in his fifties with something of the theologian sent by the bishop about him - perhaps his air of having given his soul over to a private god whose universality he sought to peddle for a living. Pulcheria, seeing them come in, decided on a tactical retreat to the far corner of the room, from which vantage point she sat watching the proceedings with absorption.

- "What d'you want?"

Angelou's voice was curt. She did not invite the two men to sit down.

- "To talk."

Hadjimbey was evidently to be the spokesman; the developer merely nodded. Taken together they gave the impression of a ventriloquist and dummy – save that the ventriloquist had dropped the pretense, and was doing the talking.

- "Talk then."

Angelou faced them squarely, arms folded across her breast. There were words in her eyes which she chose not to let reach her lips.

Hadjimbey, fielding her challenge, matched Angelou's terseness with his own.

- "Your price. To stop all this."

The voice was a low, wheezing growl. Angelou's full-throated, sarcastic laugh, by contrast, rang out energetic and true.

- "Ha, ha! Ha, ha!"

Her smile was broad, her teeth gleamed white in the dim interior light.

Hadjimbey couldn't help it; the growl grew deeper, the wheezing more impatient.

- "Damn it, woman! How much d'you want? Let's finish with it!"

Angelou was now regally calm.

- "I knew the two of you would show up like this sooner or later. Sit down. Well, sit!"

The developer sat down first, hurriedly, like a schoolchild obeying a stern teacher; then Hadjimbey settled his bulk into a chair next to the other man, but slowly, making a point of taking his time. Angelou remained standing.

- "All right. Now listen, and listen carefully. It's about Avraam Salih."

The developer looked puzzled; he turned to Hadjimbey as if for enlightenment, but the blank lenses still obscuring the older man's eyes remained directed at Angelou.

- "Avraam Salih?"

Hadjimbey's tone was disdainful, bored almost. It was Angelou's turn to feel goaded. Trying to keep her voice calm, she said,

- "You killed him - or your hired thugs did, it couldn't have been hard these days to find either Christians or Moslems who hated him and were only too glad to oblige, could it. Or let's be charitable and say it was just that you were afraid the police would think what I thought, and consider you a prime suspect. Anyway, you didn't want them to find that body, did you."

The developer was growing agitated in his chair.

- "Mr. Zenon! What in God's name?"

Angelou's smile was pitying.

- "What's the matter? Didn't you know your Mr. Hadjimbey dug up the dead body and moved it?" She addressed Hadjimbey's greenish-black lenses. "I can prove it. And don't think I'm bluffing."

The developer's face was ashen.

- "Miss Angelou! I swear! The body - killed - ! I swear!"

Hadjimbey rounded up on him with a swiftness unexpected in someone of his bulk and age.

- "Shut up! Idiot!"

- "But Mr. Zenon!"

- "I said shut up!"

The younger man was now near collapse. Rivulets of sweat ran down his forehead. He covered his face with his hands and began to moan.

Angelou continued, unmoved.

- "Nice piece of theatre, the two of you. Now here's my theory: you knew Avraam was going on television, and you knew he hated your selling the land for a hotel site. You were afraid that he'd do just what I'm doing now – use the programme to wake people up to the consequences, get them on his side. So you got rid of him. Only it didn't work, did it?"

Hadjimbey, ignoring the other man's state, kept the blind lenses of his sunglasses trained on Angelou's face.

- "What are you going to do?"

She paused. The developer had ceased to exist for both of them. Each word was slowly, deliberately enunciated.

- "Nothing. If you call the hotel off."

Several minutes passed, punctuated only by Hadjimbey's stertorous breathing. The developer, in the depths of his despair, had even given up moaning. Finally, the older man said,

- "Why?"

Angelou's voice was meditative. As she spoke she looked away, addressing an interlocutor who wasn't there.

- "Because that would be everything coming out just right."

She paused, looked at the two men. The developer appeared stunned; Hadjimbey had taken a string of amber worry beads out of his pockets and was fingering them slowly. Angelou, her voice that of a schoolmistress expounding a theorem, said,

- "Avraam wanted to stop the hotel - you killed him - because you killed him, the hotel will stop. It's perfect." She paused. "The thing is - "

For a moment, it suddenly sounded as though she might be getting ready to cry; but her voice, when it continued, had laughter in it. "The thing is - Avraam would probably have forgiven you! He was like that, you know - used to say, 'The evil are evil because it's their nature. They can't help it.' I said to him once, I said, 'And if this God of yours exists, why is there evil anyway? Why isn't there just good around?' You know what he said? He said, 'Evil is the yardstick by which we measure good; you can't have one without the other. What else is God but the possibility of good in a world full of evil?" And on and on. I said to him, 'If evil is the price we have to pay for God, then He's a luxury we can't afford!' But he stuck to his theories. He was cracked, you know, that grandson of yours!"

She looked almost challengingly at Hadjimbey; the dark lenses looked blankly back.

- "Funny - I'd never thought of him as that before. Your grandson! That's who you killed! Your own future!"

Hadjimbey's voice was virulent.

- "He was my daughter's half-Turk bastard! He was less than nothing to me! And he had no future!. As for killing him - !" He paused abruptly, shook his great bald head in rage - whether in denial, or defiant confirmation of the act, it was impossible to say.

- "Yes. He'd have agreed with you. He said to me once - it wasn't long before he died - he was standing in front of the wardrobe mirror over there and he said, staring at his reflection, 'Who d'you see, Black-Eyes?' I said, 'Don't be silly. I see you - who else should I see?' But he persisted: 'No, I'll tell you who it is - the last man of his kind. Absolutely the last.' Then he was silent for a while; then he said, 'Is there going to be another shadow theatre master after me? Is there going to be another child born to a Moslem and a Christian who love each other?' He was sad the whole evening. And he was right; there aren't going to be any more people like that. Not now."

The silence in the room was total. Hadjimbey seemed to be thinking about something else entirely, as did Angelou, who was gazing through the window. The rain was now imminent. The developer sat slumped over, abject, insignificant. For the first time Hadjimbey's voice, when it came, sounded old and frail.

- "I'll think about it."

He heaved his bulk awkwardly off the chair; the developer followed suit with the stunned air of a man emerging from the rubble of his house after an earthquake. Angelou watched them walk to the door;

she herself made no move. In the instant before the door closed on their retreating backs she said,

- "Just in case one of the things you think about is how convenient it would be if my van went off the road - "

Without turning round, Hadjimbey stopped.

- " - there's a paper in a safe place for the lawyers and the police to read, if something happens to me. That's all."

As the door finally shut with a thud, Angelou went back to the preparation of the baskets. When she had finished she carefully placed a folded napkin over each one, then carried them outside to the van. Switching on the engine, she saw the first drops of water on the windshield; the sky to the west was now black. The rain was set to last all day.

At the protest site, the women and the workers were huddled in separate groups, each furnished with a clearly inadequate number of umbrellas. The mood, near-festive during the previous days despite the underlying tension, had grown obviously sour on both sides; everybody wanted it all, somehow, to be over. Angelou's arrival with food and drink lifted spirits among the protesters a little; but, as she scanned the pinched faces of the women, Angelou had no illusions. "I'm going to start losing them," the coffee shop keeper thought to herself, "if the weather doesn't clear in a day or two."

- "Need help?"

It was Ermioni. Angelou started; the question seemed to be a direct response to what she had just been thinking. The two women had scarcely spoken since Ermioni had completed her spying mission on Hadjimbey more than a month before. Angelou missed the nurse, and then again she didn't; it was as though there were two Ermionis, the one that existed before Angelou learned the truth about her and Avraam Salih, and the one that came after. She longed for the first, but hated the second body and soul; and it was the second she was doomed to know from now on. Her answer was curt; she refused to meet the lay nurse's eyes.

- "No. 'S'all right."

Ermioni hesitated, as though preparing to say something; but the words remained unspoken on her lips. Angelou noticed that today her eyes held no blue at all - only green, a dark troubled green Angelou did not recall their having ever taken on before, flecked with grey. The moment passed; the nurse turned away, and the lanky figure merged with the crowd of women. As Angelou herself joined the group to begin distributing food and wine, she saw Ermioni out of the corner of her eye, bare-headed but walking tall despite the rain in the direction of the bulldozer sitting idle in the middle of the would-be construction site. At the rear of the machine, leaning against one of the treads, stood the ancient bicycle which had served the nurse, rain or shine, on her rounds for two decades.

Suddenly, unexpectedly, a roar sounded out; the bulldozer, for the first time since its menacing manoeuvres of the first day, heaved to life. Angelou, horror-struck, watched the driver start to back the monster, apparently prompted by the rain to shift it to firmer ground; saw, in nightmarish slow motion, Ermioni lose her balance and fall to the ground in a heap with the bicycle. For one interminable second, Angelou's vocal chords refused to yield any sound at all. When her scream, and those of the few others who had noticed what was going on, came, it was already too late.

- "Aieeeeee!"

Inexorably, the treads crushing the life out of Ermioni continued to roll as the driver sat aloft, oblivious amidst the noise of the bulldozer's engine to both the accident and the yells of the crowd, frantic and mixed with wailing by now, urging him to stop. Angelou turned away, her face in her hands; she heard the machine's rumbling finally shudder to a halt, then start up again as the driver was finally induced to shift into forward, divined from the screams and anguished shouts the macabre retrieval of Ermioni's body, heard the consultations about fetching the priest, relatives, a doctor; but looking was beyond her. Everything - everybody - was beyond her.

Automaton-like, she climbed aboard the van, started the engine, and drove back to the coffee shop. She barely got inside before her head began to spin; the room around her dissolved, and she slumped sack-like to the floor. Pulcheria, who had been sleeping on the bed, jumped down to investigate; after sniffing Angelou for a few moments she settled in a crouching position next to the inert body, and waited. When Angelou came to, the cat's eyes were the first thing she saw: turquoise eyes, the exact turquoise of Ermioni's eyes indoors, when the light that came in through the windows was that of early morning, and she was happy.

Chapter Twelve

Angelou knew me better than anyone did, but she misjudged me with regard to one thing: I would have been in favour of this protest of hers, would even have joined it if the women had agreed to have a man along, thinking that, in the end, private revolutions are not enough, and that thoughts must give way to deeds before anything can change. It would have been an error of judgement, of course, achieving only the most short-term of goals. For what is one Zenon Hadjimbey, in the face of a world full of others sharing, if not his ruthlessness, his selfishness and greed for money? Is society perfectible, when human nature is not perfect?

Ermioni was dead; the village of Ayia, for the moment, had been wrenched from the grasp of those who would destroy it in the name of helping it grow. Participants and spectators were celebrating the outcome as a victory, and so it was - for a day. The more clairvoyant - was Angelou one of them? - dared not think of tomorrow, when the men and machines and the money would simply shift elsewhere, to begin gnawing the bone of another village, in another place, whose inhabitants would surely be too complaisant or too venal or simply too innocent to pit themselves against the forces which Ayia had fought off for now.

The truth is, Ermioni's extinction was the only irreversible achievement of our little revolution.

But, I hear my own voice arguing, one must act - take a stand - if nothing else, for principle's sake. Yes, one must; the question is, act where? Act how? It has always seemed to me, my momentary enthusiasm for the women's protest excepted, that efforts at revolution are best directed inward, to overturn those human flaws which doom external revolutions each and every time they are attempted. For every single one of us to try to be better, to do the right thing; it doesn't sound glorious, there are no barricades to erect and no banners to fly. But what a changed world that would be!

Angelou, right about now in the conversation, would be on the point of hurling her brandy-glass at my head. We wanted the same things, but we never did see eye to eye on how to bring them about. "That's religion, not revolution! Spare me your God pap!" she would fume, and I would retort that her teeth weren't strong enough for the diet I had in mind. Then we'd both laugh, and she'd sing a song to cheer things up: "An Old Sea-Wolf of a Captain Goes A-Sailing", or "The Mountains Echo As I Weep". She had a glorious voice to the end; neither the brandy nor the rolled cigarettes had marred its velvet, throaty texture, as full of light and shadow now that Angelou was in her late thirties as when she and I first started keeping company more than a decade before.

All this reminds me obscurely of my father. He had waged his own small revolt against distinctions and strictures of class, race, religion, privately and with no other ally than my mother. He made nothing of it, seeming to believe that any other man in his situation would have acted likewise, that is to say defied - though ignored would be a better word - opposition and convention.

After he left for America, the only news I had of him took the form of a brief postcard, which I could count on receiving every six or eight months. The postmarks tracked a westward course through the big cities - New York to Chicago to San Francisco - and invariably carried the same message: "I have found work and am in good health. If you want to come to America I can sponsor you. I embrace you, your father." There would be an address, which I took to be that of a rooming-house, to which I would dispatch my reply - a letter, as loquacious as my father's missives were laconic, detailing the things that had happened not only to me but to all and sundry in the village since our last communication.

The cards kept coming through the years. Then, suddenly, for a year and a half, nothing; then, one summer morning, an envelope addressed to me in an unknown hand, containing a newspaper clipping dated four months earlier. The handwriting was rounded, neat; for no other reason, it struck me as being that of a woman. The printer's ink on the clipping was smudged, as though the small rectangle of paper had been fingered for a while before being sent. Under the headline "Worker Dies in Fall" it recounted, in three terse lines, the accidental death of Mohammed Salih, welder, in a fall from the girders of a skyscraper under construction.

As I read it, a curious feeling came over me, as of my body dissolving from the centre outwards; I felt an urge to go over and look at myself in the wardrobe mirror, which I wouldn't have been surprised to find empty of any reflection. Then, slowly, my flesh seemed to coalesce about my bones again, but in a subtly different configuration, so that the Avraam Salih who now stood with a dazed expression his face in the middle of the room was not the same man who had opened the fatal envelope several minutes earlier; that man was gone, like my father, and would not come again. That night, trying to philosophize away my grief, I told Angelou that the death of one's parents is a second birth of sorts; and she smiled an ambiguous smile, and didn't disagree.

I don't remember crying, then or later. Perhaps if I had, I wouldn't have dreamt the same dream almost every night for the next few years: in it, I was standing in a very high place, on a tower or a cliff-top, with the darkness and the wind about me; someone I knew but could not see was standing next to me, to whom I said excitedly, "Look!" as I jumped. But the leap was abortive; my vantage-point had been much closer to the ground than I had supposed, and instead of the long fall I had expected, I landed on soft grass in a mere ignominious moment. I would wake up, heart pounding with unspent adrenalin, a bitter taste of failure in my mouth; it would take me hours to calm down enough to go back to sleep, during which I pictured my father's fall, which must have been long, long, long. Or so I imagined, wondering what had crossed his mind during those last fatal seconds. Had my mother come to him? Had I? I also wondered about the person who had mailed the clipping. Was it really a woman, and if so, who? A lover? A kindly landlady?

Two days later, Kamenos showed up at my door, on his annual voyage to the cape. In my misery and confusion I had forgotten that I was expecting him; as soon as I opened the door, he said,

- "What's wrong? Rats eat the figurines?"

His concerned face belied the joke. I told him the story, right off. After a few moments staring at the floor, he looked up at me with pitying eyes and said,

- "So what makes you think he jumped?"

I blushed scarlet in a way I hadn't done since making a fool of myself in our early days together. The ease with which he had guessed my secret unnerved me; but I didn't deny it.

- "He'd been going west - all the time - he'd reached the ocean - the place where he fell, it was going back over his tracks, I mean east again - "

I stopped; what I was saying sounded lunatic to my own ears, but it seemed to make sense to Kamenos, who sat nodding in mute assent. He let a few minutes go by. Then he said,

- "Did I ever tell you about my father?"

His gap-toothed grin was infectious; I smiled back.

- "No. Never."

- "That's because I don't know the son of a bitch! Ha, ha!"

We were both laughing now, though in my case it had more to do with the release of nervous tension than amusement.

- "Did your mother? I mean - "

I was covered with confusion once more; but Kamenos only laughed harder than ever.

- "Guess she must've met him once at any rate! Though you can't see very well in the dark! Ha, ha!"

He had never spoken to me about his family before. I wasn't sure whether he was ribbing me, or whether there was something in this bawdy account of his origins. He read the doubt in my eyes.

- "Well, I've lightened it a bit for laughs. But not much. Want to hear it?"

I nodded, yes.

- "Not a lot to tell. My mother knew him, all right. She'd been sent to work as a maid in the town, with a rich family, she'd never tell me which one. There was a young son about her age - "

Suddenly he stopped; his face had clouded over, and there was disgust in his voice.

- "Bah! - why tell it? You recite the rest, it's easy enough!"

But he didn't let me recite it; not that I would have. Instead he continued, his voice getting louder and more bitter; he sounded as though he was declaiming the plot of a play whose quality he despised.

- "Promises of marriage! Outrage of family! Young man who never meant it anyway off to Europe! Maidservant out on her arse! Shame, humiliation, rejection by the mother and father that begot her!"

He wiped spittle from his mouth; then, with a seemingly enormous effort, forced himself to stop ranting and sat there shaking his bull's head. The big, meaty hands hung between his knees, flexing and unflexing nervously. At last he said,

- "She wouldn't get rid of it. "It": me, yours truly. Had me, and raised me, doing washing and mending. They never spoke to her again, her lot. And the others, of course not. If she'd told me who, I'd've personally wrung his neck. Yes, sir, personally. Which she knew, so she didn't. Would've spat on his money. Just wrung his neck, that's all I ever wanted to do. My father!"

Then he said,

- "It happens all the time."

The same words as Angelou. I felt more desolate than ever; but now the tables had been subtly turned, and I had become the comforter, Kamenos the one in need of comfort. I went into the kitchen and prepared two cups of strong coffee, sweet the way he liked it, and served them up with a tot of brandy for each of us. A wake for all fathers, the bad and the good. In a little while we grew merry again and spent the rest of the time till noon telling dirty jokes. Then we set off for

Angelou's to get something to eat, and discuss that evening's show.

We did "Christina and Afif", in honour of my father; all the women cried, even Angelou, who normally didn't waste her tears on made-up sorrows in plays. Only Ermioni's eyes, two sharp points of turquoise fixed on me from way in the back as Kamenos and I emerged from behind the screen, seemed dry after the performance. As we were gathering up the figurines, I heard her voice behind my right shoulder. Her lips were almost touching my ear.

- "Condolences! Are you all right?"

I hadn't seen her since the previous week; she must have heard the news from Angelou. Not for the first time, I was suddenly furious with her. My voice was a hissing whisper, but she recoiled from it as though from a cannon-shot.

- "Get lost! Don't you come near me in front of her!"

I was sure Angelou could see us, and that she would guess our secret. But when my panicked eyes scanned the room, I saw that she had her back turned serving tables and was paying no attention to the dismantling of the show. By then Ermioni was gone; looking through the open door I just made out the tall figure striding off into the night before the darkness obscured it from view.

When I turned around I saw Kamenos watching. He gave a little shrug, as if to say, "None of my business"; he never alluded to it afterwards, and I never confided in him, either about Ermioni or about Angelou. But he had found me out for the second time that day.

Chapter Thirteen

- "I tell you, Miss Angelou - the timing couldn't have been better."

Mr. Theo, long, gold-tipped cigarette between his fingers, had the look of a man whose labours are about to be rewarded. Swinging his crossed knee lightly to punctuate what he was saying, he sat relaxed at one of the coffee shop tables.

- "The programme's in less than a week. If the protest had lasted even a couple of days longer, we'd have missed the slot, and then - "

He did not elaborate on the consequences of missing the slot, but from his expression it was evident that he considered them to be pretty horrendous.

- "And you should be thinking about that offer. I mean, that Saturday night variety show has top ratings; they could get any singer they wanted. They won't wait for ever, you know."

Angelou, washing coffee-cups in the corner, ignored the second part of his speech. Her tone was dry.

- "Glad Ermioni got killed just at the right time. Know what I wonder, Mr. Theo?"

She didn't pause between the two statements. He looked a little disconcerted as he answered,

- "No. What?"

His mind was clearly elsewhere by the time she replied.

- "I wonder why anything at all ever bothered to happen before television."

He stared at her with the bright stare of a newborn infant that knows something of note is before it but cannot possibly comprehend what. Angelou, looking round from where she stood, saw his expression and smiled. She was paler than usual, and seemed thinner, perhaps the effect of the black shirt and trousers she had worn since Ermioni's burial. The nurse's gruesome death had caused a sensation; people had flocked to the funeral from the four corners of the island. The interior of the church and the churchyard could not hold the crowd, which spilled over into the streets of the village, and the flowers sent in tribute formed a small mountain in the modest cemetery.

After that, there was no question of the hotel project continuing; the developer announced the indefinite suspension of all works and decamped with all his men and machinery. It was said Zenon Hadjimbey was suing his erstwhile business associate for breach of contract, and that the developer's lawyers were invoking a *force majeure* clause on behalf of their client; but all that merely skimmed Angelou's consciousness as a leaf carried by the breeze skims the water. Avraam was dead; Ermioni was dead; the hotel was scuppered. For five days now she had juggled the three facts in her mind, now trying to make them fit together, now weighing one up against the other, like an interminable puzzle that one can neither solve nor leave alone; she felt she was condemned to it for life.

For the moment, her torment made her immune to Mr. Theo's self-absorption. Forbearingly, she said,

- "Forget it. I was joking. Want a brandy?"

He had already forgotten it before her absolution - did not even realize she had given one - and was now heading for the door. As he opened it, Angelou saw a television van pull up outside; in a few minutes a cameraman walked in, then a soundman, then a mini-skirted young woman sporting a dubious blonde mane and the generic title of "Make-Up". The hand she rested on Mr. Theo's arm was proprietary. After sizing Angelou up, she removed it, and set it to work trying to erase the dark shadows under the television man's eyes with foundation. Mr. Theo, dodging the cotton wool pad she was deploying, was issuing instructions to the cameraman. This was to be the concluding scene of the documentary, ending the story where it had begun: in the women's coffee shop, which had also furnished Mr. Theo's film with its title. Angelou said,

- "D'you need me?"

They didn't need her; they had a lot of footage of her from before and during the protest, and the close was to feature Mr. Theo alone, explaining what it all meant. Angelou, with a small mock-salute, stepped outside. She called out,

- "Pulcheria! Puss! Puss!"

She hadn't seen the cat since the previous afternoon; Pulcheria had never missed breakfast before.

Angelou kept calling for a few minutes; then, as though struck by an idea, abruptly called off her search and walked over to her pedlar's van. In a few minutes she was pulling up in the shade of the carob tree across the the road from Avraam Salih's shuttered house. Shuttered, but not deserted. In the yard, Odysseas Kamenos' battered car stood parked; and on the doorstep, Pulcheria enjoying a sunbath beside him, sat the puppeteer himself. He didn't get up as Angelou walked towards him. His eyes as he watched her approach were sombre.

- "Mr. Odysseas?"

He looked at her in silence for a moment, weighing the question in her greeting. Finally he sighed.

- "Funny thing. Until I got here I still half-expected I'd find him."

Then, as Angelou made no remark,

- "Dead is dead, isn't it? Wishful thinking, ghosts."

All the while there was something awry in his manner; Angelou was reminded of a deaf-mute, who speaks words that he supposes will hold a meaning for his interlocutor, but which he himself cannot hear. For her part the coffee shop keeper just stood there, an immobile figure in black; no longer Angelou herself, but, as at the women's protest, the personification of an idea. For a moment, Kamenos stared down at his hands, hanging enormous and idle before him. Then, with the air of a swimmer who has at last decided to plunge in water he knows to be icy, he looked straight into Angelou's eyes.

- "I know who killed him."
- "Who?"

Her voice was steady, as was her posture.

He leaned back against the faded wood of Avraam Salih's front door. He recited the story like a poem one has learned by heart, for school and not for pleasure.

- "I was mad at him, see. Really mad. I told myself, who is this snot-nose, that he should be the one to tell people on television what the shadow theatre is all about? Everything he knows, he learned from me! And what he doesn't know would take a hundred years to tell! Why him? Why not me? I thought he was ungrateful, not sending the television man to me instead. I was his teacher, wasn't I? He owed me! I cursed him - to tell the truth, I hated him. First I thought, 'I'll show him; I won't stop by before Assumption Day this year. Fuck him and fuck the women's coffee shop. Let them wait for me till they rot, I don't care!" But as the time came closer, I knew it wouldn't do. I wanted to confront him; I wanted to shame him, make him admit he'd betrayed me. I decided I'd show up on his doorstep just before dawn, by surprise; like a bad conscience, that comes up and gnaws at you just when you thought you didn't have one."

There were great beads of sweat on Kamenos' forehead; they ran into his eyes and made them sting, obliging him to stop and pull out a handkerchief from his trouser pocket. Wiping his face, he continued,

- "I drove up around four in the morning. I didn't dare come closer than about a mile, maybe a mile and a half, for fear he'd hear me too soon. I left the car by the side of the road and I started to walk to the bridge, to hide there until I could go to the house. I almost didn't see him in time; Avraam I mean. He was sitting on the parapet of the bridge, smoking; the little red point of his cigarette marked him at first, then, as my eyes got used to the dark, I could see him as well. I was just trying to decide what to do when I heard the footsteps. I lay low, and watched; it was that nurse, that friend of yours - the lanky one. He wasn't expecting her, I could tell by the way he stood up; they exchanged a few words, then I think he said, 'What's up?' Or maybe, 'Wake up', I couldn't be sure. Whatever it was, she didn't like it - started hitting and scratching at him like a wildcat. He was having trouble fending her off without hurting her. I should've come out then. I should've gone up to them and stopped it. I thought of it, I really did; then it all came back to me, why I was there and everything, and I said to myself, 'The hell with you, Avraam Salih, you can get out of your woman troubles by yourself.' If I'd suspected she had a knife! I should've gone up to them!"

Angelou still had not moved. Kamenos voice, as he continued, was slower, more agonized.

- "I crept back to the car after that. I meant to stay awake and go knock on his door around six, but I fell asleep; it was more like six-thirty when I woke up. I knew it right away - something bad lay up the road. As I drove to the house my heart was in my mouth. I saw him lying in the yard - there was no sign of her. I could tell he was dead, or as good as."

The eyes he raised once again to Angelou were pleading.

- "I was scared! If I reported it, they might think I did it - because of the television programme, and all! I mean, I did hate him - when I found out!"

He paused for a few moments, collecting himself.

- "Anyway. I drove on, to the cape. It was early, nobody even saw me go through the village, at least I think not. The cops never thought of me at all, I guess. Or of that nurse. If they really were trying to find out who did it, that is, which I doubt."

Suddenly, unexpectedly, he began to sob; his bent head revealed his bull's neck, tanned almost black by the sun. His enormous shoulders heaved. The words he spoke into the big hands were muffled and distorted by grief, but Angelou could make them out quite plainly.

- "My son! My son! My son!"

Angelou searched inside herself and found nothing to say. Yes, she thought: sins of omission are the worst. One can expiate an act, however dreadful; but how does one atone for the deed not done, the word not spoken? Yet her own words, words that might salve Kamenos' loss and guilt, wouldn't come. Her face a mask, Angelou turned around and walked back across the road to the van. All the way to the coffee shop, she heard the puppet-master weeping.

Inside, in a state of giggling excitement, Nina was preparing coffee for the whole television crew. "Make-Up" was standing next to the girl at the stove, trying to tease the dark, curly hair into a bouffant with a hairdresser's comb and laughing at the ribald comments of the cameraman and soundman, sitting at their ease before one of the tables; at another, Mr. Theo was breaking open a new pack of importeds. Seeing Angelou come in he exclaimed,

- "There you are! I was waiting to talk to you before we go!"

- "What about?"

Something in Angelou's voice made Nina push the blonde assistant aside and stop giggling. The woman, pouting prettily, put the comb away and sat down beside Mr. Theo, her bare knee almost touching his. The soundman unfolded a newspaper and began to talk football with his colleague. Mr. Theo's tone grew testy.

- "What about! About the variety show! I told you Miss Angelou - they've got to know - "

He stopped; even he knew something was amiss, now. Angelou's voice wasn't loud, but its tone caused the two men at the next table to end their conversation abruptly. "Make-up" sat frozen and wide-eyed; Nina, at the stove, dared not make either a move or a sound. Angelou lowered her face to within a few inches of Mr. Theo's own.

- "Wake up, Mr. Theo. For once in your life - wake up!"

He stared at her; his face had grown pale. As she started up again he cringed slightly, like a stray dog fearing a blow.

- "Two people died here. Two! Not ants you step on without thinking: people! People! And now, what, in your opinion? I'm supposed to go and sing on television and get rich, and everything'll be fine? Get famous and rich, and it's all just fine? *You* would have, wouldn't you? Wouldn't you?"

She had seized him by the shoulders now and was shaking him violently; "Make-Up" screamed, and the soundman and cameraman jumped up and began to wrestle Angelou and Mr. Theo apart. Nina, in her corner, was taking in the scene with wide, fascinated eyes.

- "Get out! Go show your bloody programme on television, and leave me alone!"

Mr. Theo's subordinates began gathering up their equipment with the alacrity of picnickers before an impending thunderstorm. As they made their hasty exit, Mr. Theo, in their wake, essayed to recover some dignity.

- "Mrs. Angelou - it's a misunderstanding - you're tired, and - "

- "The misunderstanding is that I took you for a man, not an ass! Out!"

They were gone, with a roar of the van's engine. Angelou, suddenly perfectly composed, sat down and began to roll a cigarette. The sweet, clinging aroma of the Turkish tobacco drifted in blue wisps towards the ceiling.

- "I need a coffee."

Nina looked down perplexed at the several cups she had prepared for the television people.

- "What shall I do with these?"
- "Pour them down the sink - what else?"

She looked at Nina as though fully registering her presence for the first time.

- "What are you doing here, anyhow? It's not my rounds day."

Though her voice was mild, the girl looked anxious. Blushing to the roots of her unruly hair she said,

- "I was walking by and I heard voices inside - your van wasn't here, so I thought - "

Angelou waved aside her explanations.

- "It's all right. Get me a coffee?"

Neither spoke for the next few minutes. As Nina set down the coffee-cup in front of Angelou, she said hesitantly,

- "Miss Angelou? Why did these things happen to our village? What you said, I mean - people dying and everything?"

Angelou didn't respond right away; Nina, thinking she hadn't heard the question, was trying to summon up enough courage to repeat it when the coffee shop keeper said,

- "D'you go to the cinema?"

The girl was nonplussed.

- "Sometimes - my mother lets me go with my brother. If there's money."

- "And in the films - do the good guys always win?"

- "Yes!"

- "And the bad guys are punished, in the end?"

- "Yes - but - "

- "Right. But. But it isn't real life. Well, our village *is* real life. No nice happy endings. Not so easy to tell the good guys from the bad sometimes, either."

Nina, pondering it all with a frown, chewed a fingernail to the quick. Then, brightening,

- "The hotel got stopped, anyway!"

Angelou looked suddenly exhausted.

- "Yes. This hotel got stopped, that's right."

- "This hotel? But - "

Angelou gave Nina a weary smile. She said,

- "Don't worry about it. I'm going to lie down for a bit. You wash the cups and go on home, all right?"

She made her way over to the four-poster bed in the corner and, kicking off her shoes, stretched out on top of the covers. As she hovered on the brink of sleep, she heard the clattering of dishes and the splashing of water at the sink; then the sound of Nina softly closing the door behind her. Kamenos' words, his ravaged, guilty face, floated through her mind. Was he telling the truth? Then why hadn't Ermioni known that Avraam's death was a murder, or that it had been done with a knife? Or had the nurse herself been play-acting when she pressed Angelou for information on how Avraam had died? The way Kamenos told it, he hadn't actually seen Ermioni stab Avraam, only supposed....Kamenos...Avraam...Ermioni...

She slept; and Avraam Salih came to her, and in the dream she was expecting him and wasn't surprised. Ermioni walked a short distance behind him; at first it seemed to Angelou that the two of them were roped together like mountain-climbers, but then the link between them turned out to be a filament as fine as a spider's web, and Avraam laughed and said, "It was a trick of the light." Then Ermioni became Pulcheria and began meticulously to bathe herself in the bright sunshine, after which she sat and stared at Angelou and Avraam with her cat's treacherous, unblinking eyes.

The dream shifted. There was a crowd of people, all on their way to Avraam's house for a performance; Mr. Theo was among them, and Odysseas Kamenos and Ermioni, metamorphosed back into her own self. Avraam and Angelou were being violently jostled by those hurrying past. As the two of them made their struggling way together along the street he said,

- "Have you seen my theatre?"

Angelou looked up ahead and saw Avraam's house; at least she knew it to be Avraam's house, but it was not the simple one-storey structure she was used to. In its place loomed an elaborate marble building in the neoclassical style, half-theatre, half-mausoleum. Avraam said, laughing,

- "My grandfather built it!"
Angelou remonstrated,
- "But your grandfather hates you!"
He laughed again; and, for the first time, Angelou noticed that he was doing it all, the laughing and the talking, without any change in the expression on his face, which was set in a death-mask. His voice and the scene began to fade; his final remark was almost inaudible.
- "He doesn't, now that he knows what's in the suitcase!"
Suddenly wide-awake, Angelou sat up abruptly; her clothes and hair were drenched with sweat. Getting up, she dragged the battered suitcase, which had stood unopened under the heavy iron bedstead since the day of its rescue from Avraam Salih's vandalized house, to the middle of the floor. She drew a deep breath. Then she raised open the lid, and began systematically to empty out the painted cardboard figures which lay inside. As she did so, she ranged them about the room; first on the bed, then, as she ran out of space, on tables and chairs; finally, on the floor itself. From their various vantage points they seemed to watch her as she delved to the bottom of the suitcase - The Mermaid, The Villain (aka Hadjimbey), The Young Lover, The Maiden, The Moor, The Lady, Alexander the Great, The Pasha, black-eyed Karagöz himself - all the creatures of Avraam's imagination, strikingly painted in bold, primary colours and fashioned with the evocative

simplicity for which he was famous among those who knew or cared about such things.

Finally, the suitcase was empty. Or almost. Angelou sat back on her heels and gazed at it: the object she had been searching for. It was a small square packet, improvised out of a single newspaper sheet folded upon itself several times and secured with a rubber band; when Angelou reached to pick it up she was surprised to find it heavy. She weighed it in her hand speculatively for a few moments, then slowly removed the rubber band and unfolded the newspaper. Inside she found a second sheet of paper, yellow foolscap this time, similarly folded into a square. Angelou resisted the temptation to tear through it, finally had it open; then she let out a small gasp. In the palm of her hand lay a three-stranded necklace of gold coins of the kind worn by the daughters of wealthy men a generation earlier; even in the half-light of the room she could see that it was exceptionally well-fashioned. Setting the necklace down she smoothed out the piece of foolscap. In the centre, penned in blue ink, she read the words: "For Angelou, when I die." It was Avraam's hand; the writing seemed fresh. Feverishly, Angelou clutched at the newspaper page which had held the yellow packet, scanned the top margin. The date could be read clearly: August 9, 1963. Two days before Avraam Salih's death.

Chapter Fourteen

I clearly hear you saying, reader: so, what's going on here? Did Hadjimbey's hired thugs do it, or was it Ermioni, or could it have been suicide after all? Or was it possibly a political killing? What kind of a plot is this, anyway?

Well, I understand your frustration; but I can only help you so far in your predicament. I am, not to put too fine a point on it, dead, the shadow of a shadow, come to the boundary between the dead and the living to help make my story known; but for me to reveal the answer to a question of life and death would be to transgress the laws governing this boundary. Who doesn't know the tale of Orpheus and Eurydice? On the journey out of the underworld, Orpheus was banned from one thing: looking round to make certain, yes or no, whether Eurydice was there.

So to tell you, yes or no, whether this one or that one is my killer - that I can't do; but I am not entirely without resources, and I won't leave you completely stranded. If I am a spirit, well, I am not just any spirit, but that of a shadow theatre master; and while I am forbidden to tell you what actually happened, I can deploy my shadow-figurines one last time, in the guise of some of the persons in this story, to show you what might have happened. After that, which ending is the right one will be up to you to decide.

And if that strikes you as unsatisfactory, unfair even, if you feel that it places a burden of responsibility on the reader which by rights should be borne by the story-teller - well, don't take it too badly, welcome it even. For it's as it should be: in art as in life, the choice of what to believe belongs, ultimately, to one's self alone.

The night of my death, I couldn't sleep. Which was apt in a literary sort of way - "I shall sleep soon, and for evermore, I need no rest now": how many romantically-dying personages in how many flowery plots have had those words put in their helpless mouths by how many hack authors? - but by no means prescient. For that matter I couldn't positively swear that I hadn't used tired words of this sort myself at some time or other - let no playwright claim he hasn't penned a single hackneyed piece of dialogue in a career spanning almost two decades. Be that as it may, that fateful night I had no foreboding of possible misfortune to come; I was far too preoccupied with the misfortunes which had already positively taken place.

Outside, the darkness was hot, humid, oppressive; the damp, coming as it did from the sea, had a salty edge to it that made the heat even more tormenting to the bare skin. The August thunderstorm which, earlier that day, had dumped great soaking parcels of water onto the parched ground, had failed to clear the air; the night was charged, electric, like my brain. My entire life at that moment seemed black: memories of my mother's early death, my father's lonely one, of the doomed white hulk of my insane grandmother, cut through me like a knife. Nor were thoughts of the living of a kind to console me: it was clear to me as it had never been clear before how my love for Angelou was a condemned exercise in self-torture, my affair with Ermioni, a triple perfidy - towards Angelou, towards Ermioni, and towards my own self.

  The image of Kamenos came to me, and I sat bolt upright in bed. The sheets were drenched with the humidity which came in through the open window, and my own sweat; I could feel perspiration covering my face in a clammy film, and my whole body was aching and feverish. A pang of conscience pierced me. What had I been thinking of, accepting that young idiot's offer to appear on television, instead of insisting that he go to Kamenos, to the source and inspiration of everything I had ever done in the shadow theatre? It was egotistical, vain, ungrateful above all; for all that I had mocked it in my head, I had allowed myself to be seduced by the notion that, through me, the shadow theatre would better project the impression that it was an art form with a future. "An art form with a future!" I sounded more like Mr. Theo than Mr. Theo himself. He and I had forgotten just one thing: reality, which dictated in terms too lucrative to be in doubt that the shadow theatre had no future. In short, gain - and, why not, art? For all that it pains penniless artists to admit it, the two aren't necessarily mutually exclusive - now lay elsewhere, in cinema, in television, in whatever else the world was inexorably evolving towards.

And I knew something else, too - something Mr. Theo, the young man of the moment, preoccupied with his allegedly blonde girlfriends and his sports car and all the other fringe benefits of his budding post-colonial career, couldn't be expected to know: that I, like the shadow theatre, also had no future. Oh, I might live a few more years - decades even! - though, in my present mood, I hoped not the latter. But I, not as a mere living, breathing creature, but as myself, Avraam Salih, an itinerant performer, a village boy, half-Christian, half-Moslem - I represented the past as surely as Mr. Theo represented the shape of things to come.

Already throughout the country, over both Christians and Moslems, the clouds were gathering; what thinking person could doubt that the "troubles" of today were a rehearsal for the full-scale civil war of tomorrow? And then, how long before someone, Christian or Moslem, pinned me to a wall with a gun to my head and demanded to know, "Are you Greek or Turk?" And when I answered, not out of heroism, but because I must, "A man!" what could they possibly do but shoot me like a dog?

And say, by some miracle of miracles, that the catastrophe failed to happen. All's peaceful; all's well. So much the better then, for my grandfather and those like him! Instead of tanks it would be their excavators and bulldozers that would wreak the destruction, levelling, uprooting, razing to the ground; we would all have survived only to become unrecognizable to our own selves. And the worst of it is that most of us would be glad of it. The rest, who viewed such a life only as another kind of death, would be a threatened - and I use the word advisedly - minority, and even that not for long.

For a moment, I thought I heard a car engine in the distance; it sounded like Kamenos' old wreck, and a brief hope rose up in me that he would stage one of his unannounced appearances and rescue me from my guilt towards him, and my insomnia. I remembered then what had slipped my mind in my misery - the feast of the Assumption was in just a few days' time. Come to think of it, Kamenos was due for a visit. Why hadn't he arrived already? But the noise I had taken for a car had died away, and no bellow of, "Wake up, you son-of-a-bitch!" came from the yard.

I gave up trying to fall asleep; got up, slipped into a shirt and trousers, and, cigarette packet and matches in hand, walked barefoot along the road to the stone bridge where Ermioni, aeons ago, had killed her snake with calculated insouciance. Because I had been thinking about her it didn't strike me as strange to see her materialize, as soon as I had sat down on the parapet and lit up, out of the briny darkness. She had always been the incarnation of some kind of darkness for me. I was exhausted; the thought of a conversation with her filled me with dread.

- "What are you doing?"

I could see the gleam of her eyes and teeth as she spoke, but not the expression on her face.

- "What are *you* doing?"
- "I want to talk to you."
- "Talk then."
- "Is that all? 'Talk then'? You've been avoiding me for months!"

I stubbed out my cigarette; I was suddenly short of breath. My voice, when it came, sounded rasping to my own ears.

- "Wake up! I'm not avoiding you. I'm not thinking of you at all. It's finished!"

As though my words had been a slap, she turned one cheek sharply away. For a couple of minutes she stayed that way; then she looked me straight in the eye and, taking a step forward, made viciously to claw my face with her nails. I saw it coming; for the next few moments we battled fiercely, in complete silence, my hands tight about her wrists, her body twisting and writhing to escape. She was taller than me, and strong. I held her off for a time; but an instant came when my grip loosened a fraction, and she lunged forward with her head and bit my left hand so savagely that I let one wrist go. She was quick with the knife then - very quick. I don't think I even knew I'd been stabbed until after I had fallen to my knees on the asphalt, and Ermioni had disappeared into the night.

I lay on the road for a while, feeling the blood sticky between my fingers, gazing at the stars. They were many, and brilliant, and quite irrelevant, now. I knew with one part of my brain that I had once loved this sky, and this peaceful little stone bridge with its white parapet and the shaded, secret places below it where cyclamen grew in April; but none of it was of my time any longer, it had all already begun to come after me.

I thought I was going to lose consciousness, but didn't; instead, I found myself crawling along the black ribbon of asphalt, which still held a residual warmth from the previous day's scorching sun, towards my house. It was not really the journey of a living being; it was the seemingly impossible progress a mortally-injured animal manages against all odds in order that it might reach the correct place to die. "How did it get there - almost dead, how was it possible?" It's a marvel to everyone, but the animal knows that it's merely a part of dying and couldn't have been otherwise. There is always life enough for that last, necessary act of will.

Once in my yard, I gave a small sigh, and died.

....

I gave up trying to fall asleep; got up, slipped on a shirt and trousers, and, cigarette packet and matches in hand, walked barefoot along the road to the stone bridge where Ermioni, aeons ago, had killed her snake with calculated insouciance. Because I had been thinking about her it didn't strike me as strange to see her materialize, as soon as I had sat down on the parapet and lit up, out of the briny darkness. She had always been the incarnation of some kind of darkness for me. I was exhausted; the thought of a conversation with her filled me with dread.

- "What are you doing?"

I could see the gleam of her eyes and teeth as she spoke, but not the expression on her face.

- "What are *you* doing?"
- "I want to talk to you."
- "Talk then."
- "Is that all? 'Talk then'? You've been avoiding me for months!"

I stubbed out my cigarette; I was suddenly short of breath. My voice, when it came, sounded rasping to my own ears.

- "Wake up! I'm not avoiding you. I'm not thinking of you at all. It's finished!"

As though my words had been a slap, she turned one cheek sharply away. For a minute, perhaps two, she stayed that way; then she looked me straight in the eyes and, taking a step forward, made viciously to claw my face with her nails. I saw it coming; for the next few minutes we battled fiercely, in complete silence, my hands tight about her wrists, her body twisting and writhing to escape. She was taller than me, and strong. I held her off for a time; but an instant came when my grip loosened a fraction, and she lunged forward with her head and bit my left hand so savagely that I let one wrist go.

The massive, determined force that bore upon both of us out of the dark with the impact of a bull knocked Ermioni to the ground. I couldn't have said whose hand held the knife blade that flashed briefly in the fray: Ermioni's, or that of the man who now pinned her down, twisting her right arm behind her back with enough savagery to draw from her a thin scream of pain.

- "Let her go!"

I had recognized Kamenos. He looked up at me; he was panting, and so was I.

- "You sure?"

I nodded; then, afraid he hadn't made out the signal in the dark, said, more loudly than I intended,

- "Yes! Let her go!"

He got up then; his clothes were dark with sweat. Ermioni, still on the ground, now lay on her side, knees drawn up, her face in her hands.

- "Are you all right?"

I didn't dare go to her; my voice and words sounded lame, and she disdained to answer me. Kamenos spat richly.

- "The likes of her are always all right! Get going, slut! Before I give you a beating you won't forget in a hurry!"

She lifted herself up then; dusted off her clothes, and, without a word, turned her back on both of us and began to walk back up the road, in the direction of the village. In a few moments she had receded into a dim, swiftly striding figure; then the figure blended completely with the darkness, and we couldn't see her any longer.

I said, not looking at Kamenos,

- "Thanks."

- "Save it. I didn't do it for you. Hysterical women give me a pain."

I looked at him then; but I couldn't make out his expression any better than I had been able to discern Ermioni's.

- "What's wrong?"

But I was dissembling; I knew very well what was wrong. His fist in my midriff knocked the air out of me completely; but, lying doubled up on the asphalt, gasping for breath, I can't say I felt great surprise.

He waited calmly, sitting on the parapet, until I'd got up before letting me see he had the knife. I said, in a stranger's voice,

- "Don't do it."

I don't know whether he realized that I meant: for his sake. The thrust was quick, almost, one might say, elegant; it reminded me of the unexpectedly deft way he had of manoeuvering the marionettes with those thick hams he called his hands. I saw him wipe off the blood with a handkerchief, calmly, then slip knife and handkerchief inside his shirt. The stab wound hurt, of course; but the only thing that really pained me was to see him turn and walk away without saying goodbye.

He wasn't walking fast. If he'd wanted to, he had the time.

 I lay on my back in the middle of the road for a while, feeling the blood sticky between my fingers, gazing at the stars. They were many, and brilliant, and quite irrelevant now. I knew with one part of my brain that I had once loved this sky, and this peaceful little stone bridge with its white parapet and the secret, shaded places below where the cyclamen grew in April; but none of it was of my time any longer, everything had already begun to come after me.

 I thought I was going to lose consciousness, but didn't; instead I found myself crawling along the black ribbon of asphalt, which still held a residual warmth from the previous day's scorching sun, towards my house. It was not really the journey of a living being; it was the seemingly impossible progress a mortally-injured animal achieves in order that it might reach the assigned place to die. "How did it get there - almost dead, how was it able?" It's a marvel to everyone, but the animal knows it's an essential part of dying, that it couldn't have been otherwise; there is always life enough for that final, necessary act of will.

 Once in my yard, I gave a small sigh, and died.

....

 I gave up trying to fall asleep; got up, slipped into a shirt and trousers, and, cigarette packet and matches in hand, walked barefoot along the road to the stone bridge where Ermioni, aeons ago, had killed her snake with calculated insouciance. Because I had been thinking about her it didn't strike me as strange to see her materialize, as soon as I had sat down on the parapet and lit up, out of the briny darkness. She had always been the incarnation of some kind of darkness for me. I was exhausted; the thought of a conversation with her filled me with dread.

I sensed the men before I saw them. In the split second before they moved in on the two of us, close enough now for me to make out the black hoods and the shotguns, I yelled,

- "Run, Ermioni! Run!"

I saw her jump over the parapet, heard the snap of branches marking her landing in the undergrowth below. The one who was jabbing the barrel of his shotgun into the small of my back said to the other two, with authority,

- "Let her go."

He stayed behind me; the others stood about five feet away, weapons at the ready. By the leader's accent in speaking the Greek dialect, I judged him to be a local man; but I didn't recognize the voice. Of the other two, one was very tall and bony, the other of average height and grossly fat. I imagined the friendly raillery as they stepped into their village coffee shop together: "There's Laurel and Hardy! How's the weather up there? That's a two-chair arse if ever I saw one!" The leader said, without easing the pressure of the cold metal on my spine,

- "Get the guy who's hiding under the bridge."

For the first time, I was aware of being afraid. The tall one moved immediately to carry out his chief's order; when he re-emerged out of the dark, he had Odysseas Kamenos with him. The puppet master had his hands up; he didn't look at me. The man behind me jabbed harder with the shotgun.

- "Your hands up too, filthy Moslem dog."

I raised my hands promptly. The fat man laughed.

- "A hero!"

The leader's tone was musing.

- "So! What do we have here? A Moslem dog-lover, and a Moslem dog. Right? Mister "I-don't-do-patriotic-stuff" Odysseas Kamenos and his apprentice - right?"

He was directing his questions at the puppet-master over my shoulder. The tall one stepped up to Kamenos and smashed his fist into his victim's jaw with enough force to knock him down.

- "Tell you what." The leader's voice remained calm, measured; he seemed oblivious to the tall one's act of violence. "I'll give you a choice."

He was still speaking to Kamenos. I could see the puppet-master's lip bleeding as he struggled up off the ground; his eyes continued to avoid mine. The two hooded figures held their guns pointed directly at his chest.

- "You see - "

The leader's voice took on the detached, academic tone of a geometry master about to explain a theorem.

- "You see - we're here to make a point. And that point is: Moslems and Christians don't belong together. They never have, and they never will. So! How do we make it?"

He paused. Kamenos was breathing hard; I knew he must be desperate for a cigarette. For the first time since I had urged her to escape, I remembered Ermioni. Would she get help? My heart hoped, yes; my brain said, no.

- "If we kill a Moslem dog, who thinks he's good enough to live with the Christians - that makes the point all right. Or if we kill a Moslem dog-lover, who thinks it's a good thing if Moslems and Christians live together - that makes the point too, doesn't it? Eh, philosopher? Does it, or doesn't it?"

He jabbed the shotgun barrel viciously into my back; my body arched with the pain. It was the first time he had spoken to me. I wondered whether he really expected an answer, wondered which answer would be most likely to pacify him. The portly one had been right: I was no hero. But his question proved to be rhetorical.

- "Take it from me: it does. So the thing is - it doesn't really matter which one of you we kill, does it?"

Something about his last words evidently didn't sit right with his companions. Passive up until that moment, they now both stirred uneasily, eyed each other through the slits in the black hoods; the tall one spoke up.

- "But Hadjim – er, the boss - he said - "

- "Shut up!" The words were a hiss. "I know what the boss said!"

The tall one swallowed the rest of his words. The leader, his authority reasserted, didn't bask in the victory, moved to end the game. Gesturing to the fat man to take over the job of guarding me, the leader stepped right up to Kamenos.

- "You or him. It's up to you."

The knife gleamed dully in his hand as he held the point to Kamenos' throat.

- "Come on! We haven't got all night! You, or him?"

Kamenos eyes' were closed; from under the eyelids tears spilled, set a course down his cheeks.

I yelled out, desperately,

- "Don't fall for it! They're here for me! Don't answer!"

The leader swung around, gave me a vicious slap across the mouth. Then, to Kamenos,

- "NOW, Goddammit! Before I slit both your throats and finish with it! You, or him? Eh? Eh?"

- "Him!"

The leader, triumphant, couldn't resist labouring the point.

- "Ha! Say that again - didn't hear you!"

- "Him!"

- "Didn't hear you, I said! Again!"

- "Him! Him! Him!"

Kamenos was sobbing openly now. I wanted to comfort him, to tell him the betrayal lay elsewhere, but found I couldn't speak. The leader's laughter held an edge of hysteria. The end was close.

- "Ha, ha! Ha, ha! What a pair of heroes! Ha, ha!"

He moved back in my direction. The thrust of the knife was quick, one might say professional; I remember thinking, as I went down, that in ordinary life my killer was probably an obliging village butcher. As if across a great distance, I heard the tall man, or maybe it was the fat man, say,

- "You're crazy, leaving the other one! He'll tell!"

And the leader, dismissively,

- "That cowardly tub of lard? He knows we'd be visiting him next if he breathed one word! He wouldn't dare!"

Vaguely, I was aware of the three hooded men marching Kamenos away. I lay on my back in the middle of the road for a while, feeling the blood sticky between my fingers, gazing at the stars. They were many, and brilliant, and quite irrelevant, now. I knew with one part of my brain that I had once loved this sky, and this peaceful little stone bridge with its white parapet and the shaded, secret places below where the cyclamen grew in April; but none of it was of my time any longer, everything had already begun to come after me.

I thought I was going to lose consciousness, but didn't; instead I found myself crawling along the black ribbon of asphalt, which still held a residual warmth from the previous day's scorching sun, towards my house. It was not really the journey of a living being; it was the seemingly impossible progress a mortally-injured animal achieves in order that it might reach the assigned place to die. "How did it get there - almost dead, how was it able?" It's a marvel to everyone, but the animal knows that it's merely a part of dying, and couldn't have been otherwise. There is always life enough for that final, necessary act of will.

Once in my yard, I gave a small sigh, and died.

....

I sensed the men before I saw them. In the split second before they moved in on the two of us, close enough now for me to make out the black hoods and the shotguns, I yelled,
- "Run, Ermioni! Run!"

I saw her jump over the parapet, heard the snap of branches marking her landing in the undergrowth below. The one who was jabbing the barrel of his shotgun into the small of my back said to the other two, with authority,
- "Let her go."

He stayed behind me; the others stood about five feet away, weapons at the ready. By the leader's accent in speaking the Turkish dialect, I judged him to be a local man; but I didn't recognize the voice. Of the other two, one was very tall and bony, the other grossly fat. I imagined the friendly raillery as they stepped into their village coffee shop together: "There's Laurel and Hardy! How's the weather up there? That's a two-chair arse if ever I saw one!" The leader said, without easing the pressure of the cold metal on my spine,

- "Get the guy who's hiding under the bridge."

For the first time, I was aware of being afraid. The tall one moved immediately to carry out his chief's order; when he re-emerged out of the dark, he had Odysseas Kamenos with him. The puppet-master had his hands up; he didn't look at me. The man behind me jabbed harder with the shotgun.

- "Your hands up too, filthy Christian-lover."

I raised my hands promptly. The fat man laughed.

- "A hero!"

The leader's tone was musing.

- "So! What do we have here? A filthy Christian, and a filthy Christian-lover. Right? Mister "I-don't-do-patriotic-stuff" Odysseas Kamenos and his apprentice - right?"

He was directing his questions at the puppet-master over my shoulder. Incongruously, I found myself worrying whether Kamenos understood the Turkish dialect; then I remembered that I had heard him speak it during stops in Moslem villages when I was his apprentice all those years ago. The tall one stepped up to Kamenos and smashed his fist into the victim's jaw with enough force to knock him down.

- "Tell you what." The leader's voice remained calm, measured; he seemed oblivious to the tall one's act of violence. "I'll give you a choice."

He was still speaking to Kamenos. I could see the puppet-master's lip bleeding as he struggled up off the ground; his eyes continued to avoid mine. The two hooded figures held their guns pointed directly at his chest.

- "You see - "

The leader's voice took on the detached, academic tone of a geometry master about to explain a theorem.

- "You see - we're here to make a point. And that point is: Moslems and Christians don't belong together. They never have, and they never will. So! How do we make it?"

He paused. Kamenos was breathing hard; I knew he must be desperate for a cigarette. For the first time since I had urged her to escape, I remembered Ermioni. Would she get help? My heart hoped, yes; my brain said, no.

- "If we kill a filthy Christian-lover, who prefers fucking Christian women and living with Christians rather than Moslems - that makes the point all right. Or if we kill a filthy Christian, who thinks it's a good thing if Moslems and Christians live together - that makes the point too, doesn't it? Eh, philosopher? Does it, or doesn't it?"

He jabbed the shotgun barrel viciously into my back; my body arched with the pain. It was the first time he had spoken to me. I wondered whether he really expected an answer, wondered what answer would be most likely to pacify him. The portly one had been right: I was no hero. But his question proved to be rhetorical.

- "Take it from me: it does. So the thing is - it doesn't really matter which one of you we kill, does it?"

Something about his last words evidently didn't sit right with his companions. Passive up until that moment, they now both stirred uneasily, eyed each other through the slits in the black hoods; the tall one spoke up.

- "But Hadjim – er, the boss - he said - "
- "Shut up!" The words were a hiss. "I know what the boss said!"

The tall one swallowed the rest of his words. The leader, his authority reasserted, didn't bask in the victory, moved to end the game. Gesturing to the fat man to take over the job of guarding me, the leader stepped right up to Kamenos.

- "You or him. It's up to you."

The knife gleamed dully in his hand as he held the point to Kamenos' throat.

- "Come on! We haven't got all night! You, or him?"

Kamenos' eyes were closed; from under his eyelids tears spilled, set a course down his cheeks.

I yelled out, desperately,

- "Don't fall for it! They're here for me! Don't answer!"

The leader swung round, gave me a vicious slap across the mouth. Then, to Kamenos,

- "NOW, Goddammit! Before I slit both your throats and finish with it! You, or him? Eh? Eh?"
- "Him!"

The leader, triumphant, couldn't resist labouring the point.

- "Ha! Say that again - I didn't hear you!"
- "Him!"
- "Didn't hear you, I said! Again!"
- "Him! Him! Him!"

Kamenos was sobbing openly now. I wanted to comfort him, to tell him that the betrayal lay elsewhere, but found I couldn't speak. The leader's laughter held an edge of hysteria. The end was close.

- "Ha, ha! Ha, ha! What a pair of heroes! Ha, ha!"

He moved back in my direction. The thrust of the knife was deft, one might say professional; as I went down I remember thinking that in ordinary life my killer was probably an obliging village butcher. As if across a great distance, I heard the tall man, or maybe it was the fat man, say,

- "You're crazy, leaving the other one! He'll talk!"

And the leader, dismissively,

- "That cowardly tub of lard? He knows we'd be visiting him next if he breathed one word. He wouldn't dare!"

Vaguely, I was aware of the three hooded men marching Kamenos away. I lay on my back in the middle of the road for a while, feeling the blood sticky between my fingers, gazing at the stars. They were many, and brilliant, and quite irrelevant, now. I knew with one part of my brain that I had once loved this sky, and this peaceful little stone bridge with its white parapet and the shaded, secret places below where the cyclamen grew in April; but none of it was of my time any longer, everything had already begun to come after me.

I thought I was going to lose consciousness, but didn't; instead I found myself crawling along the black ribbon of asphalt, which still held a residual warmth from the previous day's scorching sun, towards my house. It was not really the journey of a living being; it was the seemingly impossible progress a mortally-injured animal achieves in order that it might reach the assigned place to die. "How did it get there - almost dead, how was it able?" It's a marvel to everyone, but the animal knows that it's merely a part of dying and couldn't have been otherwise. There is always life enough for that final, necessary act of will.

Once in my yard, I gave a small sigh, and died.

....

I gave up trying to fall asleep; got up, slipped into a shirt and trousers, and, cigarette packet and matches in hand, walked barefoot along the road to the stone bridge where Ermione, aeons ago, had killed her snake with calculated insouciance. Because I had been thinking about her it didn't strike me as strange to see her materialize, as soon as I had sat down on the parapet and lit up, out of the briny darkness. She had always been the incarnation of some kind of darkness for me. I was exhausted; the thought of a conversation with her filled me with dread.

- "What are you doing?"

I could see the gleam of her eyes and teeth as she spoke, but not the expression on her face.

- "What are *you* doing?"
- "I want to talk to you."
- "Talk then."
- "Is that all? 'Talk then?' You've been avoiding me for months!"

I stubbed out my cigarette; I was suddenly short of breath. My voice, when it came, sounded rasping to my own ears.

- "Wake up! I'm not avoiding you. I'm not thinking of you at all. It's finished!"

As though my words had been a slap, she turned one cheek sharply away. For a minute, perhaps two, she stayed that way; then she turned and, looking me straight in the eyes, said,

- "She killed your child. I helped her do it."

For a moment, I stared at her as though she had spoken in a language foreign to me; her words made no impact, were nothing but a jumble of odd sounds. Then, in a small corner of my brain, they slowly began to assume an awful meaning. I said, through lips suddenly parched and dry,

- "What child? What are you talking about?"

But I knew with a horrible certainty what she was talking about. She spelled it out for me with eyes gleaming green in the moonlight, and a small, malicious smile.

- "You slept with her, once - right? Well, she got pregnant. Didn't tell you, I'll bet. She told me, though. I know about herbs and things. She asked me to help. Saw her through it - the bleeding, and the pain. Made sure there wasn't an infection, afterwards."

The malevolent smile was still on her face as I turned and vomited over the parapet. She waited for it to be over; I knew she had more to say.

- "She told me she loved me, when it was over. 'Only you, Ermioni!' It was a torment to her, the thought that I might leave her because of it all. I let her think it. Stupid bitch! Stupid, blind bitch! And you loved her! You bastard! You loved her!"

She was crying hysterically now; her nails made to claw viciously at my face. For the next few moments we battled fiercely, my hands tight about her wrists, her body twisting and writhing to escape. Suddenly the fight went out of her; as I released her she sat down heavily on the parapet, her face in her hands. She stayed that way for a few minutes, then stood up to face me. I thought she was going to attack again and braced myself; but she just spat in my face, turned around, and walked away. I stood watching her, feeling the wetness of the spittle on my cheek and lips, as the darkness swallowed her up. Then I started back towards the house. I don't remember getting there; when I next became aware of what was happening I was sitting directly on the ground in the yard, with my back resting against the stone rim of the well. Judging by the stiffness in my joints when I tried to move, I must have been in that position for some time.

    I wasn't in any doubt as to what had to be done. Ermioni's story might be the spiteful fiction of a woman scorned, or the truth - it hardly mattered. The moral was inescapable and the same: there was no future in my love for Angelou - quite simply, there was no future. Whether Angelou had really torn my child out of her belly, or whether she absolutely rejected the notion of ever bearing a child of mine, which of course she did, it was all the same. The result - and Ermioni knew this! - in either case was simply this: I, Avraam Salih, had reached the end. This was the end. I myself had known it, too, for some time. The other day, wrapping up my mother's gold necklace for Angelou, the idea had been lurking, unacknowledged, at the back of my mind. Just tidying things up, I had told myself; just putting things in order that had been lying around in a mess for too long. Just getting, I now realized, ready to die.

    I stood up, walked inside, reached into a kitchen drawer, found the knife I wanted; went back outside, drove it in hard, with a remnant of strength threw it into the well. The last, thin thread of consciousness in me thought it discerned, at the edge of the yard, the burly figure of Odysseas Kamenos; then it lost interest in living beings, fixed itself for an instant on the stars, on my house, on the little stone bridge under which cyclamen grew in April, on all the things I had loved once, but which had already begun to come after me.

    I gave a small sigh, and died.

Chapter Fifteen

It was a dark evening in December. The women's coffee shop was full; Angelou, no longer in black, sat as usual slightly off to one side, studying her patrons over the glass of brandy in her hand. The women's mood was sombre after the six o'clock news on the radio - Angelou was still resisting television, even though the men's coffee shop had one by now. The bulletin had been dire with accounts of political trouble. Fighting between the Christians and Moslems was now general over the island; neither the approach of Christmas nor of Ramadan seemed likely to deter the combatants, who had been looking forward to this showdown for some time. The revolt of the women of Ayia against Hadjimbey's hotel was forgotten, as was Angelou's women's coffee shop, the existence of which as revealed in Mr. Theo's documentary had excited such comment. It was the men's day, now.

Angelou looked and looked at the women, as if their forms, their faces, might provide the answers to the questions throbbing in her mind. Was it fair to think of men as destructive, women as peacemakers? Avraam had been a peacemaker, the very opposite of destructive. For that matter, a woman might have been his murderer. But weren't he and Ermioni merely the exceptions that proved the rule? Or was the so-called rule in fact merely a nonsensical generalization?

She took a sip of her drink, shifted to a more comfortable position in her chair. It was true – wasn't it? - that all through history, it was men who had held the power and determined events; and what was history, but a sorry account of competition and lust for power, of wars, tyranny and destruction? But suppose that, in some way scarcely imaginable, women had somehow been in the position of power. Would they have used it more wisely? Would a women's world be a world of harmony, instead of strife?

No, that was too simplistic, surely, thought Angelou. Give women power, and they, too, will become its creatures, ready to perpetrate any evil to expand or preserve it. Her mind shifted again to Avraam, to his notion that artists and women were privileged among human beings in creating something, as he put it, where before there was nothing. Maybe that was the answer then: insofar as life was hope, hope lay with women, who literally brought forth life - who gave birth to the Avraam Salih's of this world. But then, the men with the guns out there killing each other daily in the name of religion and country - they were mothers' sons, too! Not only saviours, but also tyrants, could emerge from a woman's life-giving belly.

Angelou tossed the remaining brandy down in one gulp. The course her thoughts were running was beginning to make her oddly happy. The next idea that rose up in her mind gave her an extraordinary sense of being with Avraam again; she could almost swear he was in the room. It's up to each one of us, she said to herself. Man or woman, it doesn't matter; we are all human beings, we all more or less have the same flaws and temptations, internal and external, to combat. Whether we fight them, or give in to them - whether we do good, or evil, is a matter of individual responsibility and choice.

As though her thoughts had been a cue, the coffee shop door opened and Xenia, Mayor Leonidas' daughter, came in, carrying in her arms a tiny white bundle. Unnoticed, Pulcheria the cat slipped in through the door after her, swept briefly by Angelou's chair, then jumped onto the four-poster bed and settled down to survey the scene through half-closed green eyes.

For a few moments, all conversation ceased; like sunflowers to the sun, the women's faces turned towards the newcomer and her fragile cargo. Xenia, beaming, sat down and delicately drew back the fluffy white blanket to reveal the exquisite little ear and sleeping profile of her month-old baby daughter. The light falling on her face and the cooing talk of the women who began gathering round to have a look awoke the baby; she searched for her mother's features among the many others hovering over her with slightly unfocused black-currant eyes, found them. Then, taking fright at the crowd of strangers observing her, she screwed up her miniature face into a mass of pink wrinkles and began, piercingly and with conviction, to cry.

The women laughed, drew back; Xenia rocked the baby to comfort her, meanwhile releasing a full, white breast and placing the nipple in the infant's mouth. Soon nothing could be heard from Mayor Leonidas' grand-daughter but contented suckling sounds.

- "What are you calling her?"

The question came from Katerina. Before Xenia could answer, Elenara said, with a gold-toothed grin,

- "After whichever one of the mothers-in-law wins! Eh, Xenia?"

All the women laughed anew; Xenia looked discomfited. Blushing, she said,

- "Yes, I mean - my husband says it should be his mother, you know, Maria. But - "

She hesitated, as if unsure how her audience would take what she was about to say next. Then, looking round, she saw Angelou's eyes fixed on her. As though the fact gave her courage, she said, addressing the coffee shop keeper alone,

- "But I think she should have a heroine's name. I mean, men get named after heroes, don't they? Achilles, things like that? Why not women?"

- "A heroine!" Liza picked up the conversation. "What kind of heroine, anyway? Women don't do brave things and become famous!"

The flush on Xenia's face deepened; but she stuck to her guns. Still facing Angelou she said,

- "Yes, they do! What about Ermioni? She's famous, for stopping the hotel and everything - she was a heroine, wasn't she?"

Angelou looked back at Xenia with black eyes grown expressionless; her mind seemed to be elsewhere. Then she stood up. As the mayor's daughter stared at her in confusion over her failure to answer, Angelou said,

- "Wait a minute."

With the women's eyes on her, she walked to the four-poster bed in the corner, felt under the mattress. Pulcheria, her eyes fully open now, watched her mistress unblinkingly but didn't move. A small packet in her hand, Angelou walked slowly over to Xenia and handed it to her.

- "Call her Constantia. It was Avraam Salih's mother's name. The necklace was hers."

Xenia, the baby cradled in one arm, laboriously unfolded the packet with her free hand. She was the first to realize what was inside. The young mother's disbelieving gasp was followed by cries of amazement and admiration from all corners of the room as she held the three-stranded gold coin necklace up to the light.

- "Miss Angelou! I can't accept this! Are you sure?"

The expression on Xenia's face was almost one of fear. Angelou, still standing next to her, smiled.

- "I'm sure. It's mine to give, and I give it to you. Just call her Constantia, that's all."

Xenia examined the necklace this way and that, reassured enough now to begin appreciating the treasure. A small smile played on her face as she murmured to herself,
- "Constantia!"
Then, turning to Angelou,
- "What did she do?"
Angelou gazed at the baby, asleep once again. All the women fell silent, waiting for her answer. At that moment Pulcheria bounded off the bed and began to rub insistently against the coffee shop keeper's legs; Angelou picked the cat up, scratched her behind the ears. For a few moments purring was the only sound to be heard. Then Angelou spoke.
- "The right thing," she said.
Down the street, two men walking home after the evening news on television heard the muted din of voices and laughter coming from the women's coffee shop and halted for an instant, trying to make out what it was all about; but they were too far away, and anyway not that interested. One shrugged, the other shook his head; then, straining to keep their bearings in the winter darkness, they continued on their way.

~finis~

About the author

Andriana Ierodiaconou is a Cypriot author, poet and former journalist. She is a graduate of The English School, Nicosia, and St. Hugh's College, Oxford, where she obtained a degree in Biochemistry. She then left the science track to follow a passion for writing. She is bilingual in English and Greek and works in both languages. Her poems and short stories have appeared in a range of literary magazines and anthologies in Cyprus and abroad. 'The Women's Coffee Shop' is her second book. Her debut novel, 'Margarita's Husband', appeared in 2007. She is married and has a son.

Printed in Great Britain
by Amazon.co.uk, Ltd.,
Marston Gate.